THE CATCH

by

Charmaine Gordon

Vanilla Heart Publishing
USA

The Catch
by Charmaine Gordon

Copyright 2013
Charmaine Gordon

Published by: Vanilla Heart Publishing
www.VanillaHeartBookAndAuthors.com
10121 Evergreen Way, 25-156
Everett, WA 98204 USA

ISBN: 9780615792545

10 9 8 7 6 5 4 3 2 1 First Edition

First Printing, April 2013
Printed in the United States of America

Dedication

The Catch is dedicated to the ones I love best: daughter Amy, grandest granddaughter CassidyRae, youngest son Paul, and my husband, Don. Thanks for your patience and understanding as I wrote *The Catch*.

Acknowledgements

And where would I be without the firm guiding wisdom of Kimberlee Williams? Thank you for showing me the way and restoring my confidence during a bad patch. I couldn't ask for a better friend, publisher, and editor rolled into one.

A shout out to Chelle Cordero and Melinda Clayton, two Vanilla Heart authors always willing to lend a hand. Thanks, my friends.

And to the Hudson Valley RWA, it's a pleasure being a member of this group of published writers.

Chapter 1

The woman in his bed sat up and shoved him hard. "Time's up, handsome."

Tom Donnelly rolled over and blinked awake.

"My name's Vicki in case you've forgotten."

He attempted his winning grin; it didn't work. *Vicki.* No Vicki came to his muddled mind. The fog lifted to recall speaking to an escort service for a date.

Naked, Vicki stalked to the bathroom with an armload of clothes picked up on the way. Five minutes later, money in her tight fist, Vicki came running out of the bathroom to scream in his face. "The deal was a thousand dollars. I count five hundred. Where's the rest?" Hands on voluptuous hips she glared at him.

Head pounding from the world's worst hangover, Tom staggered out of bed and lurched to his dresser. *Money hidden somewhere under...* Clothes flew as he searched and came up with a roll of cash. Face flushed, he handed her four hundred fifty dollars. "Sorry. I'll make it up next time."

"Loser. Word gets around, no one's gonna go with you. Not from the best service in town." Vicki slammed the front door.

Tom shook his head. *Happy New Year to me. Sunk so low I had to hire a date for the big party. Me, the catch, every girl's hope reduced to this.* He fought the first impulse to go back to sleep. Disgusted with himself, Tom stretched his athletic body under the covers and cursed. "Another New Year and what have I got to show for it?" Shelves of trophies gleamed in the shadowy darkness. Framed photos of past glory and diplomas hung on the wall. Only Charlie Costigan, a girl from long ago, mattered and now she was unattainable. Thoughts of Charlie and blood surged directly to his cock.

Throwing off the blanket, Tom sat up pressed his head with clenched fists overcome with a sense of failure and somewhere in his mind he heard the sound of a gavel hit followed by a deep voice saying, "Guilty. As. Charged. Tom buried his face in a pillow to stifle out-of-control-sobbing. *No need to wake neighbors and spoil their New Year day. Yeah. Thomas Donnelly. Always a thoughtful guy. My epitaph.*

Chapter 2

The bathroom cabinet contained sleeping pills. *An easy way out. A glass of vodka to wash them down. And peace. Better than the gun in the drawer next to the bed. Big brother Patrick would hate him.* Shaking hands, a gift from the hellish hangover, and he fumbled opening the bottle of pills. Tiny clicks as small capsules cascaded over the counter onto the floor. Take one at night. The safe instructions encouraged him Take more—a lethal dose. Warning: Do not drink alcoholic beverages while taking this product.

Tom arranged the capsules in a row then automatically rearranged them into a formation. The corners of his mouth tugged into a smile. They looked like a football formation made of pills. He pictured the play to come next. First a scramble for position he--the quarterback—called for. A winning strategy ended in another touchdown.

One quick motion and the capsules were flushed, a part of sewage in the great city of Chicago. *As for me,* Tom straightened, *there's nowhere to go but up.*

Wrapped in a blanket Tom hunched over a legal pad and wrote. RESOLUTIONS FOR THE NEW YEAR. I, Thomas Donnelly do swear to myself the following:

Make work the first priority. More billable hours. Take all the continuing ed courses demanded by the partners. *Patrick warned I was heading for a fall with all the womanizing and carelessness and now me, the younger gifted brother was on the brink of disaster.* Fingers ran through shaggy blond hair, Tom made a note to get a decent haircut and begin again.

The Catch

Apologize to the immediate family today. Make amends. AA. Can I stop drinking without help? I believe I can. I'm not an alcoholic. Yet me, the catch with everything going had nothing today. Not too late to build a career, find the right woman and start a family.

What brought me to this day? A set of circumstances lined up before him. The New Years Eve party when Charlie said she intended to remain a virgin. His first refusal from a girl might have begun his decline. *Geez! So egotistical.* And slowly he proved every girl targeted became a happy partner under him. With a few drinks, more girls, football, and he began a slow descent.

God forgive me. What a fool and over a girl's choice; a special girl who said no. No one to blame but me.

The page had room for more but Tom wanted to wash away last night's stupidity and start fresh.

Under the needle-like shower, Tom welcomed the sting and hot water. Charlie showed up in a flashback. Never far from his thoughts, the only thing he knew was she married the nerd, Jerry Kahn, now a boring CPA for God sake. He cleared his mind the way he'd done at least a hundred times before football games. *Focus.*

Dressed in a tattered NU sweatshirt, sweat pants and running shoes, Tom pulled a knitted purple cap over his ears and ran three flights down to the street. He hadn't kept up with exercise, like everything else good for him, but this was the first day of the rest of his life. He laughed at the great cliché. They were words to live by, a vow he intended to keep.

Living in the Old Town section of Chicago turned out to be a good place to run. He found a park nearby with a running track, passed a high school with another track, and streets were almost empty on this January 1st. Not too cold on this first January morning and he loved the puffs of frost coming from his mouth as he breathed. A few runners waved and called Happy New Year. Nice. He didn't know anyone, so wrapped up in his own life, and that too would change. His parents needed some encouragement to know their kid wasn't a failure after all. Yeah, today's the day to make amends.

Chapter 3

A big Irish feast at his parents' home scared Tom. He squared shoulders strong and wide and rang the bell to the modest old house he'd grown up in. Lace curtains still hung in the windows. Through the bay windows the familiar sight of a Christmas tree with garlands of pop corn all around, candy canes on branches and home-made ornaments brought an ache to Tom's heart. The German Shepherds he'd grown up with lifted their old heads and tails wagged at the sight of him. He knew inside the house smelled like everyone's favorite, corned beef and cabbage. Laughter, music and delicious aromas filled the air. Bridget Donnelly flung open the old door and hugged her baby son.

"Tommy, me boy. So pleased to see you t'day. I cooked your favorite. Can ye smell it?"

"Yes, Mum." It broke his heart to see the way she forgave his terrible behavior. He gazed into a face so like his own; slightly turned up nose, high cheek bones, clear blue eyes. The square jaw came from his father. Pop's voice bellowed from the kitchen. Tom shuddered. He'd have a lot to account for this first day of the New Year.

A tall burly man with a ruddy complexion, Pat Senior sliced corned beef like a pro and why not? Years of experience, several times a month as chief volunteer at the local soup kitchen, and now a retired cop. Always active, the stern father disappointed in his errant youngest son called to Tom. "Grab a cold one and an apron, Tom. Set the table. Your mum needs help, she does."

Tom flushed at mention of the apron; a family joke about anyone who failed to hold their liquor. "I'm on the wagon now, Pop, thanks. I'll tend to the fire." He headed outside to the wood pile and stomped through falling snow to load logs into a wheelbarrow. An axe stuck in a huge stump. Tom hung his jacket on a branch, freed the axe and practiced swinging. He loved the whistle of air, the power he felt connecting as splinters flew. Before long he'd chopped enough logs to last his parents for the winter. A shovel stood behind the door reminding him of days when his job included cleaning the walks.

Wet snow perfect for snowballs and snowmen clung heavily to the old shovel as Tom scraped the path. Physical labor felt good as Tom's mind and body re-established a healthy rhythm. A bag of Ice-melt-away lay unopened in a corner just inside the door. He ripped off a corner, carried the bag outside and spread crystals on the walkway vowing every time snow fell, he'd do this chore for his parents and be grateful.

He deposited some logs inside the back porch, heard a commotion at the front door and knew his brother had arrived. One quick wash in the small bathroom at the back and Tom made himself presentable. He hurried to the bright living room where Pat, arm around a gorgeous girl, stood smiling.

"Hey Pat, Happy New Year."

A darkly handsome Patrick beamed, his five o'clock shadow already showing. "Tommy, good to see you, bro. Meet my fiancée, Melanie Callahan."

Tom's first thought was Wow! What a shape on this chick and she's going to marry lucky Pat. An instant later he realized how shallow his thoughts were. Yeah, a pretty Irish girl and he hoped his brother made the right choice. In the next few minutes, Pat revealed the fairy tale about his girl. Melanie moved to Chicago from a small town in Missouri and struck it big time when a modeling agency spotted her. Melanie Callahan became featured bride of the year and Patrick, for the first time, was in love. They sparkled together and their parents reflected their joy. Happy about the news, Tom had a surge of envy and then felt a sense of strong resolve to improve his status.

Aunts, uncles, and cousins Tom hadn't seen in a long time showed up for the feast, everyone bringing a specialty like Mincemeat and pumpkin pie in triplicates. Tom helped serve, played with the kids, and at day's end, after the last goodbyes were called, he asked his family to sit for a while. They gathered by the crackling fire, Mom's weary face showed her age and Pop's eyes narrowed at Tom, a question mark in his expression. Patrick, arm around Melanie, leaned forward with full attention on his younger brother. Tom's heart filled with love and hope. He cleared his throat.

"On this first day of the New Year, I want to tell you, my dear family, that I'm turning over a new leaf to begin a better chapter in my life. I know I've disappointed all of you. This time, I'm determined to become the son and brother you were proud of in the past. Talk's cheap, I know and you're probably looking at me and thinking, "So put up or shut up," but I'm not a kid anymore. I will prove to be worthy of your love."

Flames flickered and died on the last log. Sparks flew touching the grate to sputter out.

They sat still and quiet for a moment 'til Pop broke the silence. "I'll drink to that, boy o'mine."

Patrick joined in."Me too, brother."

Mom cried and Melanie smiled.

The Donnelly's began a New Year with good news.

Two days later after a full day at work, Tom headed to St. Margaret's Church where his dad volunteered at the soup kitchen. Eager to see his father, Patrick Sr. in this role and possibly get to know him better, Tom hurried up the wide stone steps of the church and stepped into a forgotten world. As an altar boy once, with church every Sunday along with classes during the week, memories rushed back to fill his heart with unexpected joy.

He followed the signs sniffing aromas of cooked vegetables and meat and figured beef stew was the main course. A whiff of cake or brownies poured into the room when the swinging doors opened. His mouth watered. He entered wide open doors to a large room filled with long tables and lines of people; there were parents with small kids, their little ones perched high on what appeared to be tired shoulders or they sat in strollers, and seniors shuffled along with trays in their hands.

So this is Pop's soup kitchen. I've heard about it for years and never once offered to volunteer. Forget your own hunger. These people need food now.

A smiling Pop ladled a generous portion of stew on a plate, added two biscuits and placed it on a tray held by a pale thin woman. "Mary, he'll be better next week, you'll see." The woman nodded, a faint smile on her face and she moved to the next table.

"I'm here to volunteer, Pop." Tom's Dad glanced sideways and grunted. His tough poker face didn't show emotion.

"Roll up your sleeves, Tommy. Grab this ladle and do a good job. Don't be stingy with portions. I'm off to the kitchen to get some more." He poked his son in the ribs. "Good to have you here."

When the last person walked out and doors closed, the volunteers gathered to eat. The feeling of belonging to this small community satisfied Tom. He sprawled in a worn over-stuffed chair, balancing a plate in one hand to mop delicious brown gravy with a biscuit held in his other hand.

A knife clinked against a glass. Tom noticed everyone paid attention because Patrick Sr. was obviously the man. "Listen up. The new volunteer is my youngest son, Thomas. He's a lawyer with Bancroft Law and Associates and tonight, Tommy rolled up his sleeves and ladled 'til his blue eyes almost bugged out. So let's give thanks and welcome to the lad."

Shouts of welcome filled to echo back in the high ceiling cavernous room.

Surprised and happy, Tom waved to the volunteers. Setting the plate down, he stood and grabbed his dad in a tight hug. "Thanks, Pops. You showed me the way."

Chapter 4

Continuing education classes were available in the evening and on Saturday. After a long day at the law office where Tom worked, he catnapped for 30 minutes, picked up a sandwich and bottle of water and hurried to the snow covered campus fighting the bitterly cold wind off Lake Michigan. One night, head down he bumped into a young woman. Her brief case went flying.

"Sorry," He raced to retrieve it. When he returned, a gloved hand reached out and both the woman and case were gone. He admired her long strides in high heeled boots and wanted to catch up but she disappeared through the doors and all he remembered was long dark hair under a red winter hat.

Two months went by and suddenly crocus appeared pushing yellow and purple flowers into view. A few times Tom caught sight of the woman, always from a distance, stride unmistakable, dark hair loose, no longer wearing a red hat. Their paths didn't cross. He figured she must be taking a different law course but with his new agenda, work came before women. Curiosity got the best of him one evening and he followed her from a distance all the way to a classroom. She sat toward the back and when a guy ran toward the same class, Tom stopped him.

"Do you know her name?"

"Oh yeah. She's hot and smart. Her name's Joanne McKenna Friedman. She won't give you her number. Doesn't date. Just studies and works." He opened the door and hurried to a seat.

Huh. Doesn't date. Wonder why. Tom loped to his building, pleased he'd made an effort to find the intriguing Ms. Friedman. He got a good look at her this time and liked what he saw. Dark eyes, the long straight hair and sleek body almost too thin yet she appeared to have muscle tone. Strong from the look at those endless legs. *Oh man, get your head straight. Time for learning.*

Three months later:

Hair slicked back as if she'd see through the phone, Tom dialed Charlie Costigan Kahn's number and cleared his throat. A strictly business voice answered. He asked for Charlie, said he was an old friend. Name? Thomas Donnelly, he said. She said please hold. No music, just a void. He thought she cut him off until at last, Charlie's voice.

"Tom, hi. Are you all right? Last time we met you weren't well."

She had a memory like an elephant, he recalled and winced. Last time he looked like shit on the downslide of his career and she was zooming to the top with her construction business.

"Hey, Charlie, last time I was in the midst of a stupid patch and now I'm climbing up the ladder not to fall again." He forged ahead checking his notes. "The reason I'm calling is I'd like to help in some way with Haven. My law firm wants all the lawyers to get involved in community affairs and I remembered your project. I have time on weekends to teach kids to play football or read or wherever you need an able bodied man to jump in."

After a long pause, Charlie spoke. "Well, Tom. That's really kind of you to offer. I'll have to talk it over with Shelley, of course. You remember my roommate, don't you? Shelley's the gorgeous basketball player your parents objected to when Patrick loved her. They didn't like the color of her skin as I recall."

"Ouch, Charlie. I had nothing to do with that. Please don't lump me in with their prejudice."

"Hmm. Sorry, Tom. You were always in a class by yourself and you were kind to me, in high school...a long time ago." He heard her take a breath. "Shelley's the manager and psychiatric social worker at Haven. Leave your number with Joanne and I'll get back to you. And Tom, I'm glad you called. Great to hear from you." And again the void. Then the impersonal voice of her secretary or receptionist came back.

"Your phone number, Mr. Donnelly."

He recited the numbers where Charlie could reach him, home, office, cell. "Call me Tom." She hung up. Well he broke the ice and if she didn't call in a few weeks, he'd call again. Maybe take Charlie out for lunch if the tight ass Joanne let him in the glass tower where Charlie was kept.

Chapter 5
Charlie

After knocking on Charlie's door, Joanne went in. "I've got something on my mind, Boss. Can we talk for a sec?" With a sigh Charlie, about to leave, perched at the edge of the desk. "What's this about?"

She sat opposite Charlie. "This Donnelly guy, he loved you and maybe still does. Am I right?"

"No way, Joanne. That old romance lasted a week. We were kids. I'm married happily with a daughter. He's looking to help out. Maybe make amends for acting like a fool years ago. No big deal." She crossed to her young capable office manager. "You don't trust anyone, do you? Joanne didn't answer. "Maybe someday you will. Trust is important."

Joanne shook her head. "People don't forget, Charlie. They carry a grudge and might find a way to interfere with your happiness."

"Not Tom. He's basically a good guy."

"You're too trusting, Boss. I'll watch out for you." And Joanne left head held high.

Odd little duck worries about me as if I can't take care of myself. Little does anyone know except for my brother, Jimmy, I've been on my own since forever. After brushing auburn hair back into a clip, Charlie rolled blueprints into a case and called to Joanne. "Time to lock up and go home." No answer from the efficient Ms. Friedman; a hand wave sufficed.

23

The Catch

Joanne was a woman of few words. Once again Joanne put in more hours than the boss lady and reminded Charlie of the way she'd conducted business in the early days. Probably her right hand person had studying to do. She always took a class to self improve. When Joanne came to C. Stuart Construction without much of a resume, Charlie had a hunch about the younger woman, sensed the hunger in her belly to succeed just as Charlie had when she was only fifteen. So far so good after one year of steady progress, Joanne was now her office manager. Charlie headed for the elevator outside her office and called her best friend and sister-in-law, Shelley.

"You'll never guess who called yesterday."

"Spill. I don't have time to play guessing games. The boys will be home from school and the girls have play dates." Shelley Jackson Costigan smoothed her new maternity tee shirt over the baby mound. "I'm busting my britches here, Charlie. Jimmy laughs when I take off my clothes at night."

"That's the prob, girlfriend. You're always naked when he's around so...Any way, Thomas Donnelly called. That's who."

"What?"

"Yeah. Remember when you said I broke his heart when I broke up with him and I said he only wanted to break my cherry?"

The friends laughed at the shared memory.

"You learned from your mother's bad example. All guys want to get laid. And you were so right to wait 'til Jerry came along. How is he? Jerry."

"Compared to before? Improving. I think."

"Takes time and a lot of patience, Charlie."

"I'm learning." They were quiet for a moment.

"So what did Tom want?"

"He claims his law firm expects the lawyers to extend a helping hand to the community so he thought maybe we needed help out here at Haven."

"But doesn't he work in Chicago? That's where volunteers would be newsworthy. Not here in little old Fairview."

"I thought the same thing, Shel. Why here? I think I smell something rotten in Denmark."

"Like ulterior motives."

"Uh huh."

"On the other hand, give the hunk a chance. Maybe he has pure motives in mind."

"Ya think?"

"Gotta go. The wheels of the school bus go 'round and 'round right up the hill to my door. As we used to say, girl friend, later for you."

Charlie strode out of the building on Lake Shore Drive into the fading June sun and hailed a cab. Time to go home to husband Jerry and daughter Emma, the two loves in her life.

Chapter 6

"Honeys, I'm home." Emma came on the run auburn curls bouncing, to jump in her arms.

"Mommy, I made somethin' special for you today. We cooked and I stirred and stirred and sorry my shirt got chocolate all over."

Inhaling her daughter's scent of pudding, shampoo, and finger paint, Charlie laughed. "I hope you brought some home for dessert." Emma wiggled down to plant small sandaled feet on the terrazzo tile, her impish smile full of mischief.

"Just a li'l bit, mommy. Daddy had the first taste and he loves chocolate."

Emma skipped down the spacious hall, her Labradoodle, Apricot wagged close behind after giving Charlie a hello lick.

The comfortable two story house smelled wonderful and why not Charlie thought. Kerry, the all around chief cook and bottle washer, joined their staff when Charlie's business grew and she didn't have time to prepare meals. No biggie since she didn't know much about cooking and didn't care. On Kerry's days off, Aunt Eleanor made sure catered meals arrived on time. What a remarkable support system available day and night ever since Charlie arrived in Chicago fifteen years ago, an unknown niece welcomed with open arms. And now she needed them more than ever. She, Jerry and Emma needed them.

Dropping her briefcase in the home office, Charlie hurried to greet her husband. She found him in semi darkness, eyes closed, head slumped sitting in the family room, a book fallen to the floor next to his chair. Tears sprung to her eyes. *No. Be strong.* "Hey, my sweetheart." She picked up the book, looked at the title and frowned. A biography. A best seller about a man who committed suicide.

Her husband of five years opened sad eyes. With an obvious effort, Jerry Kahn, successful CPA, re-arranged his features into a smile. "Hi. How was your day?"

"Good. We have a new customer. Actually it's a spread north of Chicago. He plans homes, a golf course, the whole thing and we've out bid the competition. The main thing is he asked Jimmy to design the project so this is truly a feather in our business." She kissed him full on the mouth and tasted chocolate. "Emma spooned a bit of dessert, did she?"

"Guilty as charged."

"Are you hungry?" Appetite diminished since the accident, he shook his head no, something he did every time she asked. "Kerry made your favorite. Matzo ball soup and brisket for Friday night."

"Will you light candles?"

"Uh, no, love. I'll leave that to your mother. Now let's go in. The dinner bell just rang."

The whirr of his motorized wheelchair stayed behind Charlie as they negotiated a turn down the hall to the dining room. She knew Jerry hated for her to see him sitting, incapacitated since the accident. During dinner, she'd break the news about a change.

Emma sat, hands in her lap, Charlie knew the expression on her little girl's face; always ready to laugh at the world at any given moment. A smart golden child, Emma had a lot on her little princess plate with daddy in a wheelchair, no longer capable of playing horsey back and other fun games. Kerry bustled in with the first course, her shiny black curls tied in a red ribbon, blue eyes twinkling.

"Yea, Grandmother's matzo ball soup."

"Thanks to Kerry. Smells delicious and thank you."

"Me pleasure, Ms. Charlie. Comin' next is tasty lean brisket with vegetables. Good for all of ye."

When color retuned to Jerry's wan face, Charlie decide to announce breaking news. "Now summer vacation is here, we've been invited to join our family at Haven. Emma has her cousins, the beach, a great house to live in, and you and I can conduct business right from there." Before Jerry could object, Charlie continued. "If you need to see clients, Robert can chauffeur. He's been asking what he can do to help." Jerry opened his mouth to speak but Charlie hurried on. "Honey, Robert's been my close friend since I was fifteen and moved in with Aunt and Uncle. And he's their chauffeur and handyman like forever. Please consider this generous offer."

Emma, bouncing up and down in the chair, clapped her hands together and Apricot barked. "Yes, yes, yes. Cousins. I love them. Let's go but first, can Kerry serve the chocolate pudding?"

Chapter 7

Full dark outside and in the quiet home, Charlie tiptoed out of bed with one thought in mind. Call Shelley.

One ring and Shelley said, "It better be good or you're in deep doo."

"Sorry. This is a big favor but Shelley, we need you. Presumptuous of me but I'm packing for a summer vacation at Haven. I know you don't have clients now. I found Jerry reading a book about a man who committed suicide and I'm scared."

Charlie heard the rustle of sheets and shh sounds as Shelley left the room. "Oh, Charlie. Of course come here. But you need an expert and I'm almost due."

"No. You're the one with insight so read up on Jerry's disability and subsequent depression. Call Nino Schiano for physical therapy. I want my man to be strong again. His mind is good, sharp as ever and arms work. And Shel, I want another baby soon...before."

"Before what?"

Charlie took a deep breath. "Jerry's not interested in me anymore. He's turned away like he doesn't want to live."

"That's understandable since he's not the man he used to be, Charlie. I'll work with him and you might need someone to talk to. Hey, you mentioned Tom and what a good friend he was when you were in high school. When he comes up, see if he's grown into a person you can confide in. A guy friend.

You're tight with Jimmy. Best brother and sister I've ever known. Consider talking to him."

Charlie sighed. "I'll think about it. Take care of yourself, Shelley. We need you and don't forget, I read about delivering babies. Not to worry. You know me."

"Brat. You and your photographic memory. No wonder you were the roommate with top grades."

"Jealous. I studied while you pranced around the hottest freshman at NU." They laughed at old memories and sobered to the immediate issue.

"It's a deal. I'll begin research tomorrow morning. Haven will be ready when you arrive. The cleaning crew comes early, Gram shops while Marina herds the kids and generally rides shotgun over the property. I'll talk to Nino, tell Jimmy and we're set."

"Thanks, Shelley, for so many things, especially being here for me. For us."

One more call. Charlie glanced at the clock. From what Joanne had told her, she stayed up late.

"Joanne, do you have a life? Why are you up this late?"

"Hi, Charlie. Studying. Waiting for your call, boss lady. What's up?"

"Studying what? I've been meaning to ask. Somehow you led me to believe it's self-improvement but that's not true, right?"

Charlie heard a deep sigh and knew she was about to hear the truth from her right hand girl.

"I've been going to night school for years toward a law degree. And Charlie, I'm almost finished and I've paid for school by myself."

"No support from your parents?"

An awkward pause Charlie recognized and didn't like it. Truth or a lie. "No. Poppa died and mother didn't care much. I want to be like you. Independent and strong and I want to do pro bono work to help people who can't afford counsel."

"Hmm. Noble but who will take your place in my company and when? I need you now. This sucks, Joanne. I'm bitterly disappointed." Charlie paced the floor, wished for coffee, tea, guidance. As someone who kept the darkest secret of all shared only with her brother, she knew Joanne told her half a truth.

"Calm down, boss. I've lined up someone you're gonna love. Meanwhile you called so you need me. As I said before, what's up?"

"Smartass. Don't ever tell me to calm down." Charlie paced a bit longer. "You've heard me speak of Haven in Fairview, north of Chicago, what you city girls call the sticks. Well, tomorrow my little family and I are going there for the summer and you will be required to travel north, expenses paid, at any time so I can juggle care of my family and business simultaneously."

"Oh. Okay, boss. I'm in. As long as I have time to study..."

"How about this?" Charlie interrupted. "I get a driver for you and you study in the car when necessary. And we communicate by phone, you fax info, keeping it all simple as possible."

"Cool. This will work. And thanks for not being angry."

"Who said I'm not angry?" Charlie disconnected. Exhausted she crept back to bed, slid in beside her beloved Jerry, prayed her suspicions were wrong and went to sleep.

Chapter 8
Shelley

Organized chaos reigned at Haven the next day. Two sets of twins were off to play dates while Haven was scrubbed clean, aired out, and made ready for the Kahn family. Groceries were put away, Shelley's grandmother had every burner going in anticipation of company plus her super special chocolate chip cookies baking. Marina Flores, hired to care for the first set of twins four years before, stayed on as a member of the household. Today she also picked Gram's tulips and daffodils to brighten the living room.

Shelley locked the office door and studied online about spinal cord injury. She gathered notes on depression to get started: a normal component of adjustment to the injury; lowered quality of life; sometimes depression was seasonal; hope considered to be an important coping strategy; goal setting; focus on progress. These were topics to discuss with Jerry and she knew his injury was in the lumbar vertebra L1-L5. Called complete loss of function in hips and legs.

Head in hands, Shelley almost cried. God she hated to research this fast never dreaming Charlie would drop their problems in her lap suddenly. All the months since the accident when she wanted to jump in, Charlie said no. Let the expert specialists in Chicago take care. Now Jerry was out of the hospital, conducting his CPA business as before with changes, of course. He worked from home, tired easily, and Charlie needed her. One thing for sure, she'd never again let her best friend down. The first and only time she'd done that almost ended in disaster. Now she wondered why she didn't spill the beans about getting pregnant with Jimmy. She'd learned the hard way to tell the truth as it happens and to teach the kids to be truthful from the time they're small. Somehow she'd help Jerry Kahn come back to his Charlie.

Just then the babies in utero rolled over. Placing both hands on her belly, she spoke in a soft southern drawl almost forgotten. "Hey, y'all. Ya think Mamma's gonna do good for her ole bud, Auntie Charlie? Wha's that? Uh, huh. You betcha, ah sure will. Now hush. Mamma's got lotsa work to do." With a smile on her face and renewed energy, Shelley continued to research.

Chapter 9

Tom sat up straight and confident as he placed a call to Charlie's company.

The cool voice he remembered so well answered brisk and all business.

"C. Stuart Construction. How may I direct your call?"

"Hi. Tom Donnelly here. I'd like to speak to Charlie Costigan."

"She's not available."

"Wait. Don't hang up. I'm an old friend and I want to be of help at Haven."

"Well, she's there but you need an appointment."

Tom hung up. A perfect Saturday in June and Charlie was accessible. A chance to talk. An apology, an explanation formed in his head. A quick Google check for information about Haven in Fairview, Illinois, and he knew how to get there. Gathering footballs and equipment little kids would enjoy, Tom dressed in old NU gear and headed north.

Joanne called Charlie and when she couldn't reach her she locked up the office and ran for her car. *I made a big mistake to reveal the boss's location to this guy.* Joanne didn't trust him no matter what Charlie said. Her long dark hair trailed back like a jet stream in her red second hand convertible as she cut through traffic and got on Edens Expressway. Again and again she tried to reach boss to no avail, message going to voice mail. At a stoplight in Evanston, she called again.

Breathless, she said, "Boss, Tom Donnelly is on his way to Haven. Sorry I let it slip."

"Easy, Joanne. Tom is coming here?"

"He said he wants to help and..."

"Okay. Settle down. Where are you?"

"Evanston."

"Great. And Joanne, don't worry about Tom. I'll take care of him."

If the boss said she'd take care of him, she'd do as promised. Joanne conjured up images of what taking care meant to a tough woman like Boss. Maybe a gun to Tom Donnelly's head as a warning or a rope hog-tying Tom the way Jimmy Costigan captured a killer at Haven a while back before Joanne joined the team. What a family. She'd miss the energy, the adventures with every construction project. Sighing, she pulled off at the Fairview exit and navigated shortcuts to Haven in hopes of beating Tom Donnelly there. He had a head start but her GPS knew the way.

Down the private road Joanne drove, a trail of dust clouds rose behind her car. After living in Chicago for so long and now to be on a road Boss owned, she thought *"Dorothy, looks like we're not in Kansas anymore."* Laughter mixed with wonder at the mystical Disney-like woods. Wild flowers were a feast to her citified eyes where smooth concrete and flowers in containers sufficed. Ancient trees formed an arbor, protective and mysterious. A quick glance to the right and there was a winding path up a hill to a sprawling ranch style house. *This must be Jimmy and Shelley's place with two sets of twins. Haven, here I come.*

Someday I promise myself I'll have everything just like Charlie. Against all odds, I'll make it happen. Joanne parked behind Charlie's truck and hurried in. One sniff of cookies and her mouth salivated. Home baked cookies and so much more with a pot of something on the stove and a rotund lady stirring round and round.

Without turning her gray curly head, Jane Jackson, Shelley's grandmother, said, "Got a few chocolate chip cookies for you, Joanne. Charlie told me you'd come flyin' in, hell bent 'n rarin' to go."

Joanne raced through the kitchen, one thing on her mind. She had to find Charlie. "Uh, no thanks. A guy didn't get here before me, did he?"

"Tom Donnelly? No"

"Great." Briefcase in hand, Joanne followed voices down the hall passed an office, unique spacious workout room, and assorted bedrooms. Open suitcases were strewn on beds, dresser drawers left open, and closets agape. The trail led outside to a basketball court and playground fit for a huge park. And Joanne, dressed in spiked heels, short slim skirt and tailored blouse, felt out of place with jocks running around bouncing balls.

"Hi. I've come to, uh, help."

Charlie ran over. "You came to warn me against the evil Thomas Donnelly, didn't you?"

"He's on his way. I called and called..."

"Not to worry. The cavalry is here. Make sure to greet Jerry, he's in the shade with Emma. Anything from the office?"

"But, Charlie, I'm worried he'll..."

"Say hi Jerry and Emma. I'll deal with Tom. I'm sure he's here as a friend." Joanne shook her head. She'd do anything for Boss and nothing urgent came up this Saturday to bother her. She pasted on a smile to cover sadness before reaching Jerry and Emma. They read a Dr. Suess book together, Emma's auburn hair back in a pony tail, faces close with her little girl self on his lap.

"Hi. Sorry to interrupt your story time. Oh, I love The Cat in the Hat."

Emma's sweet voice piped up. "Can you stay? My daddy's a great reader." Plump toddler arms spread wide to show how great.

Jerry's smile didn't touch his eyes but she saw the effort. "Hi Joanne."

"Thanks for inviting me. Emma, I have to help your mom with some work. If I have time, I'll be back."

The Catch

Damn, she rushed here for what? Charlie wasn't worried so why did it disturb her? When she'd answered an ad for Charlie's construction company last year, the place was disorganized. Joanne came in for an interview and it was love at first sight. Given full reign after showing capability, Joanne became part of the company. Soon she'd leave to pursue her law career but right now, what Charlie asked for, Charlie got.

Deflated, Joanne wandered back in to watch for the guy who should be arriving any moment. She couldn't resist hanging up Emma's clothes, one ear down the hall for footsteps.

Size 4T sundresses too cute for words; sneakers with sparkles and Velcro closures, sandals in every color and Mary Jane's all to be placed on a shoe rack.

Bending over in the closet, Joanne heard a familiar voice. Ice formed in her veins.

"Charlie, you in there? It's Tom here to help as I promised a while ago."

Bumping her head against a pole in the closet, Joanne stood up fast and turned. There he stood, the infamous Mr. Donnelly.

"Oh. You're not Charlie but I've seen you before." He squinted getting a better look as Joanne pushed past him, her long dark hair flung back. "Yes. On the campus at night. By accident I knocked your briefcase away and ran to get it for you. After that I caught sight of you many times. I guess you're in a different class."

She gathered her case, looked around the room to make an escape and warn Charlie.

"What exactly is it that you want here, Mr. Donnelly?"

He laughed. "Why so frosty and who are you to ask such a question?"

"I'm Charlie's right hand person at C. Stuart Construction, the one who answers the phone and keeps the riff raff out."

"So you're Joanne. I pictured an older woman. Much older. And you, well," Tom took a deep breath and slowly exhaled, "you..."

With a hand gesture down the hall, Joanne said, "Wait in the living room. I'll tell Charlie you're here. She's very busy." Heart pounding, Joanne turned and strode out the back to the playground. This was not in her job description.

"He's here." Joanne crooked a finger to her boss in mid leap toward the basket. Charlie cursed like a drunken sailor.

Shelley held her bulging stomach and laughed. "Girlfriend, I win. The winner gets a trophy."

Her husband Jimmy carried a squirming Labradoodle puppy, while everyone clapped and yelled.

Towel around her neck, an animated Charlie almost danced down the hall. Joanne couldn't believe her eyes. Friendly. Boss was actually friendly toward this guy. This was not a good sign from what she'd heard about Mr. Donnelly, the womanizer who once loved her boss. Rumor or truth?

"Hey, Tom. We didn't expect you so soon. Today's moving in for the summer day and our annual basketball competition. Let's talk for a minute." They went out to the gazebo and sat.

"Do I pass? Inspection?"

"Hmm. I want to make sure of your motives for driving way up here to please your law firm. I can't see publicity from helping at Haven."

Tom smiled. "Still straightforward, Charlie. You see right through me except this time my motives are pure. I don't care about publicity. All I intend to do is lend a hand with the kids, teach football, sportsmanship and be a friend the way grown-ups are for each other. Let me prove myself, please."

A grasshopper hopped over Tom's big sneakers to land on his knee. Cupping his hand he captured the big green insect. They had a stare down. Tom let him go and looked up to see Charlie holding out her right hand. Grateful Tom shook hands with his old love now a friend.

Joanne peered out the door watching as they approached the house.

"Tom, you're dressed for action with the kids and they're always ready for sports so c'mon back and get reacquainted. Hey Joanne, meet Tom Donnelly, this is Joanne McKenna Friedman. Joanne's the office manager at our company."

The Catch

Tom extended a hand Joanne ignored. Noting this Charlie said, "Handshakes are not Joanne's thing. She's cautious about well—everything."

"I hung up Emma's clothes. Save them for me. They'll be considered vintage by then but I love them. Didn't get to finish because uh, he showed up."

"Thanks for the help. Otherwise, I might have shorts and a tee for you and I think new sneakers close to your size. We still get suppliers sending sneaks. Pays to be a jock. Stay for dinner unless you have a date."

Chapter 10
Tom

Tom watched the intimate exchange with envy. Charlie always had a way with people making them feel comfortable. He used to with ulterior motives. Now he wanted to become more natural, make friends with women and men. He followed Charlie out to the back of Haven where he said hello to Jimmy and Shelley, now Charlie's sister-in-law, more beautiful than ever glowing with pregnancy, a cluster of small kids around them. Jimmy as a father, the tall kid from nowhere, Charlie's brother, who became a well known architect. They shook hands.

See what you can accomplish when you set your mind to it, Tom thought. *And Shelley Jackson, a girl from Mobile on scholarship, now a VIP in charge of Haven. And how she played basketball! A dream to watch.*

Charlie led him to a shady area where a man sat in a wheelchair, a little girl the image of Charlie on his lap. *Oh my God. Jerry Kahn. Her husband.*

"Tom, you remember Jerry Kahn, my nerd from NU? We're married and this is Emma. They are my dearest loves in all the world." She leaned down, lifted her husband's chin and kissed him. "Emma, say hi to our friend, Tom. He can teach you to throw a football today. Won't that be fun?"

Tom put out his hand and Jerry surprised him with a powerful handshake. Then came the dainty sweet light touch of the small child with Charlie's smile.

The Catch

Overcome with emotion, Tom sunk onto the bench next to Jerry and Emma danced away with her mother. Jerry removed his glasses to polish them. Slowly he breathed on first one lens and then the other, using a cleaning cloth to wipe away the fog. He nodded and replaced the cleaned glasses.

"You're thinking poor Charlie. Her husband handicapped, no longer the man he used to be. How can I, Tom the great catch from long ago, help." Tom didn't meet his eyes. "Look at me. Tell the truth. I can handle it. It's nothing compared to facing my reality." .

Tom met Jerry's steady gaze. "Yes. All true..." His voice trailed off. "You've got one helluva a handshake, Jerry." Tom flexed his fingers. "Physical therapy?

"Forced upper body training. You should see my pecs." A cynical laugh. "I'm more developed than...before. Never had to be. But I didn't think about the handshake. Really?"

"Oh, yeah. I bet with a little, uh, with a lot of work you can play basketball or tennis and that's where I can help. Think about it. You don't have to sit in the shade all the time."

Tom, the jock, watched Jerry, the nerd, bounce the new idea around in his computer savvy brain.

"Not interested." His eyes turned a steely brown. "You seem fit and healthy, Tom. Not far removed from the jock I knew." Again they shook hands. Again Jerry displayed his powerful grip and Tom moved on, right hand aching. He recognized Jerry Kahn as the formidable CPA whiz he'd read about. The one all top guns in Chicago turned to. Something unnerved Tom. He also sensed a familiar hopeless quality about Jerry; to a much lesser degree one he'd overcome not too long ago.

Chapter 11
Joanne

Joanne decided to finish what she'd started by hanging up clothes in the master bedroom. Curious to know what happened when Tom met the family, she hurried and didn't change as Charlie suggested since she had to study. Maybe she'd stay for dinner then split. This seemed like a good safe plan. One glance out the window and there was Tom surrounded with little kids, his blond hair sun streaked already and summer had just begun. Beach bum. She scowled. Yet the kids were giggling and rolling balls around the court. Two boys, twins with Charlie and Jimmy's auburn hair tried for baskets set up to their height. Dainty Emma ran up to the hoop and tapped the ball in. Laughter and "no fair" rang in the air. What a time and in the midst of it all was Tom Donnelly. Her fists clenched. Look at the fraud working his way into Charlie's beautiful family and Haven. *I must be nuts*, she thought. *Why can't I let go of distrust and anger? Charlie's so easy with people, so forgiving. Shit. I'll get an ulcer with all the poison inside me.*

Jimmy and Shelley's grandmother set up a long table and carried baskets with rolls, carved meat and vegetables until the games stopped, everyone lined up to wash at the outdoor faucet and the dinner bell rang. Inside, Joanne entered the spacious bathroom and opened her briefcase empty of files and business papers in there. Today she carried a secret stash of special make-up. After careful skin cleansing with little pads removed from a zippered bag, Joanne used a cover-up to hide one scar on her neck, another under her chin and touched up her make-up. Always look your best, a personal mantra. Last she brushed straight hair 'til it shone and strode out. *Eat and run,* she thought. *Make a quick getaway.*

"Hey Joanne, I thought you'd split. Pull up a chair, have a carrot and feast." Charlie loved to tease her because she had a small appetite and never ate much. "Gram's cooking is the best."

An unoccupied chair at the end appealed to Joanne. Good for escape. She sat, gazed around and suddenly the enemy tucked in next to her. *Why did she feel trapped by Tom?* Pass this and pass that and soon Joanne found her plate filled with far too much food smelling oh so heavenly. One small bite of beef tenderloin led to another and soon in her mind's eye she pictured herself as a hungry little girl, mother saying, " two bites is enough for the likes of you, kid." Forcing the picture away, Joanne slowed down, chewed slowly and ate with the same deliberation that led to all her accomplishments.

Aware of Tom's glances and attempts at conversation, she ignored him instead choosing the company of little Jake and Luke Costigan, Shelley and Jimmy's boys. Smart and funny, the boys had twin sisters age three and Shelley expected another set of twins this summer. They tossed conversation over her head like a basketball to their new best friend Tom. Positive they wished Tom sat next to them, Joanne offered to switch chairs but Tom seemed to enjoy her discomfort. Finally, before dessert, she kissed the small boys, said goodbye, whispered to Charlie if she needed her Sunday, Joanne would come at a moment's notice.

Briefcase in hand, Joanne strode to her car. A deep voice caused her to stop.

"Cookie for your thoughts."

Tom held out two chocolate chip cookies wrapped in a napkin. "What have I done to make you so antagonistic toward me?" A frown creased his brow.

Trapped she thought fast. "Don't flatter yourself. I'm cautious about uh, new people coming close so thanks for the cookies. And, and don't ever hurt Charlie or her family. Ever. Or Thomas Donnelly, you'll have to answer to me."

She drove off hair streaming, tires churning a cloud of dust billowing behind.

Chapter 12
Joanne

Family. Mind pictures of family contrasted with her own invaded Joanne's thoughts on the drive back to her small apartment in Old Town. The joyful scene at Haven with kids, friends, and family; a long table and no squabbling over food. Growing up with an indifferent mother who cared about the other kids and not the little one, the after-thought as Joanne was called. She got lost in the shuffle and had to scrape for herself. When Poppa died, she ran away from the nowhere town to find work in Chicago. The only thing she knew was to clean and cook so she wound up in a diner. The nice guy didn't ask questions, just handed her a big apron that wrapped around twice and when he pressed against her, she punched him. "No funny stuff, mister, or else." He laughed. Then one night a man who looked like a teacher, came in and … Months later she ran for her life. Beginning again with dirty money, Joanne McKenna Friedman needed work and a real education.

Old Town was a renovated beautiful section just north of mid town Chicago. Joanne parked in her designated space, removed her Smith &Wesson from the glove compartment and slipped it in her pocket. Full dark now although the private lot had lights, uneasy she still required protection. Cautiously she moved along at a brisk pace, noting bushes in full bloom needed attention. A major trim to prevent someone from hiding would accomplish that. Although the huge Magnolia tree near the entrance to her building was beautiful someone could hide behind it. Spiked heels going click, click on the pavement announced her arrival. Next time she'd change to sneakers.

The Catch

The doorman greeted her, his pleasant smile a beacon of comfort but Joanne wouldn't release her grip of the Lady Smith in her pocket until she entered and checked each room. Hours of training taught her to be cautious with a capital C.

Behind multiple locks at last Joanne felt safe and lonely. Joanne thought about dogs; the Labradoodles were so affectionate and easy to train. Or cats. Cats couldn't protect you. She'd find out more about a dog, one she'd take to work. No law firm would allow a dog especially to a newbie unless she had a handicap. How about my special need as in scared to death since... No Joanne. Get over yourself.

With care she hung up her expensive skirt, wiped dirt off the gorgeous shoes that caused daily pain and set her white shirt, bra, and panties aside to wash. The pistol kept her company from the white tile counter. A hot shower came next, the big shampoo and rinse and now she sat on a ledge in the shower and dried with a fluffy white towel. White for purity, she thought inspecting a few burn marks on her side. Bikinis covered most of them. Oh well. Nobody's perfect. Dry skin soaked up creamy lotion as Joanne lathered her legs and arms. Memories of a man she'd made the mistake of trusting rushed back and she dropped the bottle of lotion. It broke and spread to soak into the grout of white tiles. She, who never cried, cried. Only the gun bore witness.

Chapter 13
Tom

Tom stayed at Haven to pitch in with the clean-up. For the first time his efforts were for something other than himself. As he gathered the equipment he'd brought for the kids, Charlie came by.

"Jerry mentioned your kind offer to help him learn basketball and possibly tennis all from his wheelchair. Thanks. He might take you up on it. Of course his P.T. maven will have the final word."

"He's a great guy. And lucky to have you." Embarrassed by the word lucky, Tom shook his head. "I'm an ass. Sorry. Poor choice of words."

She grabbed his arm and squeezed. "We are lucky. We're fortunate he's alive. The car was totaled and he has his mind and upper body intact. This summer Nino will help him work on the rest. Knowing my husband's strong reserve, we expect," she hesitated, "good results."

Charlie turned away but not before Tom saw tears in her eyes.

"Hey, on a different subject, why is Joanne such an icicle when she sees me? I get frosted you know what's when she looks at me."

"Hey yourself, have a leftover cookie or two for the road and I'll clue you in on Ms. Joanne."

They sat outside in old wicker rocking chairs cleaned up for another summer. Lake Michigan breezes cooled the starry

The Catch

June air already perfumed with Jane Jackson's flower beds. The companionable setting helped Tom and Charlie return to a lost friendship.

"First of all, Joanne's a loner. I've never heard her talk about dating or friends. Odd for a beautiful young woman to be so isolated by choice I believe. Actually Joanne's been with my company one year and now she's about to take the Bar exam. But she's intense about me for some reason. Maybe because I gave her a job on a feeling I had. Damn, I hate to lose her. She's got a replacement lined up." Munching on a cookie, Charlie grew quiet.

"That's it?"

A nod from Charlie. She rose and stretched. "Long day and a whole summer ahead. Thanks again. Feel free to call me directly if you want to come up again. Maybe we could talk about old times."

Tom had a lot to mull over on his way back to Old Town. In the past, he'd be edgy and search for a bar with a woman for the night. Since his resolutions made January 1st, his mind had cleared to find a path open different from the mess he alone created. Joanne McKenna Friedman intrigued him. Stand offish, hostile, as loving to people she knew and trusted like a trained guard dog. What makes a person like that, he wondered. A set of circumstances set her on a straight road and he wasn't allowed in. Not acceptable. He'd have to find a way to tear down the wall so she'd let him in. *Play your cards right and by summer's end, just maybe Joanne would melt. Sincerity? He could fake it. Oh no.* He turned into his apartment complex, a step up from the old one, and parked. *Absolutely not. That's the old Tom finagling your way into a woman's bed. This time you be a straight arrow and let fate and honesty work magic.*

Chapter 14
Shelley

With all the cousins off to the beach under Marina and Gram's supervision, Shelley invited Jerry to her office for the first consultation. As old friends, this would be delicate. In digging deep into his accident and subsequent injury, she discovered interesting facts. His spine at L5 had radiculopathy, compression on the nerve. Also an existing condition of spinal stenosis showed bulging discs. Before the accident, Jerry seldom complained about lumbar back pain radiating into his legs causing sciatica. It was possible that the trauma caused major bruising of the spine and a shift of discs already out of place. Emotionally, the always controlled Jerry Kahn, was responsible for the single car accident and may have turned against himself as punishment. Hysterical paralysis of the legs? Psychiatrists would consider the problem and delve into his subconscious to find the source. Shelley's experience as a psychiatric social worker might help Jerry. Recalling one sleepover at Charlie's aunt and uncle's elegant home on Lake Shore Drive when they were seventeen, Charlie commented on Shelley's ability to see into and cut through all the secrets. Whatever seemed to scare Charlie back then didn't stop her from setting Shelley on the right career path. Time to roll up her sleeves and get to work.

"Jerry, might you be more comfortable outside in the gazebo? The office is cozy but on a day like this, well it's your choice."

"Comfortable? Shelley, I'm not comfortable anywhere since..." He gestured toward his legs, eyes downcast, shoulders slumped.

"Outside it is. Lead the way." Gathering her note pad, pens and a thermos of iced tea, Shelley waited 'til he was forced to take the lead. Her clever husband Jimmy had built a wheelchair accessible path to the outside. Jerry's muscular upper body got him up and outside and she watched him take a long moment to breathe in the sweet summer air.

"This is good, Shelley. Glad I thought of it." A hint of the old Jerry returned. "Okay, shrink me. I'm ready."

An attempt to stifle a laugh didn't work and Shelley cracked up. "Nicely put." Now for the hard part, she thought. "Go back to the night of the accident. The icy weather, road slippery. Like that."

Sweat broke out on Jerry's forehead. "I uh, can't." His hands shook. "No, can't go back there."

In a low soft voice, Shelley spoke to her friend. "Close your eyes. Picture your state of mind. Were you eager to get home to Charlie and Emma, a hot meal, the fireplace warm, the little Labradoodle on your lap?"

"Exactly the picture I see. Exactly." Tears streamed down his unshaven cheeks. "My fault. All my fault."

She tried to pull him back and couldn't. Maybe they'd done enough for now. She gave it one more try. "Jerry, Charlie doesn't blame you. Emma doesn't blame you. It wasn't your fault. Accidents happen. Say out loud, it's not my fault. It's not my fault."

His chin and mouth set in a rigid line.

Shelley continued. "It's not my fault, it's not my fault."

He softened. "It's not? Are you sure? You weren't there. How do you know?"

"I know you, Jerry Kahn."

"You know what I know?" His words poured out in a rush. "This I know for sure. My wife needs a whole husband. Not half a one."

Shelley had no idea this was on Jerry's mind. Oh dear God. "Let's take a tour around the area. You haven't seen all the improvements we've made." They drank iced tea and moved away from the gazebo. The wheelchair whirred away up and down the path with ease.

Shelley tucked her papers in a folder and left them to retrieve later, pleased with the short session. The first Braxton Hicks contraction hit hard, slowed and went away. *Not again.* She hoped they wouldn't be part of this pregnancy like the others. They were exhausting and she had so much to accomplish. She paused to catch her breath and waited. Babies shuffled around to add to her discomfort. Once the contractions began she had to time them.

"Wait up, Jerry. I'm not as fast as I used to be. Not now."

His wheelchair slowed and turned. "Are you all right?"

Another one hit too soon. "No." Where could she sit? They hadn't installed enough benches.

Jerry showed up close to her. "What?"

"Just premature labor pains. I've had them before." A vine covered boulder nearby seemed like the perfect place to sit. Carefully Shelley made her way, step by step and perched, cold and uncomfortable but at least off her feet for a few minutes. She checked her watch and prayed for another few weeks.

"I don't have a phone handy. We should call someone." Jerry pounded the arm of the wheelchair. "I'm the one to help and I can't. I just can't."

"Calm down. We both must calm down. I will get through this and Jerry, I believe with all my heart, you will too. Last night I dreamed you got out of the chair and walked. Not too steady but you walked."

With a sad shake of his head, he frowned. "Pipe dream, Shel. Let's get real."

She rose, gathered strength without the intermittent pains, and placed one foot in front of the other to reach Jerry. Together they made their way back to Haven. "Keep thinking it's not your fault, it's not your fault. And Jer, I have a lot of ammunition to fight what you have. Get ready."

He shook his head. "No wonder you were a champ at NU. You never said no. Charlie told me." A white butterfly landed on his shoulder.

"Yeah. She meant I never said no to the guys I dated. Basketball. I had a scholarship and do or die was my motto."

Before lunch, Nino came for Jerry's physical therapy. She'd talked to Nino about working Jerry's leg's to keep them in shape. The worst fear was atrophy. They agreed with what various machines to use and physical hands-on care plus continued upper body strengthening.

With Jerry in good hands, Shelley stretched and finally packed it in for a needed nap. The next sounds she heard were high pitched voices calling Mommy, Marina and Gram saying hush and dogs barking. The digital clock showed 4 p.m. Shelley sat up dazed and hungry. *What in the world will I do with more babies to care for?* "Be right there," she called and got ready to face the evening.

Chapter 15
Two weeks later
Charlie

Martha Lundquist entered C. Stuart Construction to meet her new boss, Charlie Costigan Kahn. Unescorted by the young woman who recommended her, Martha was in for a surprise.

"Ms. Lundquist." Charlie greeted the older woman, smile wide. "She said you're terrific and I have a feeling..."

"You're Charlie? I expected someone much older." She blushed. "I mean..."

"Why Martha, I do believe you're funny and I never cut funny. So let's get to work." She gestured to Joanne's desk, neat and orderly. "Get familiar with what's happening here then buzz me with this button," gesturing to a red one on the phone, "and we'll go on from there. And screen my calls but we'll get to that after. Be friendly, pleasant, sincere."

"I can fake that." Martha sat, adjusted the chair and opened a drawer.

Laughing, Charlie strode to her office and closed the door where her mood changed. *That Joanne. Dumping a brand new employee to walk in alone. Sure Martha has a good resume, better than the one Joanne showed me a year ago but what the hell. We both deserved a better beginning than this. Now I have to show her what's what while my ex-employee studies for the Bar exam. I'd like to break a bar over her head.* Charlie paced wearing a trail through the beautiful new high pile hazel green carpet with her boots.

Green the color of her eyes, Jerry said when he picked it out. Before the accident...

A call to Shelley assured her Jerry was doing better. "Better than what?"

"I'm working on something totally different with him, Charlie. An idea from research found on the Internet and it's exciting. All I have to do is convince him..."

"Difficult to do, Shel. He's a mule."

"And with the Braxton Hicks..."

"Oh no. Make sure you have a phone handy."

"Well, we were caught short the first time."

"We? You mean you and Jerry?"

"Uh, gotta go."

Oh God. I've got to tell Jimmy. Her phone buzzed. Martha on the line. "Ms. Charlie, I'm ready for more anytime you are."

"Come to my inner sanctum and I'll show you the ropes."

Interrupted by phone calls all day, Charlie told Martha not to worry. She'd get the hang of work at a busy construction office soon enough. Over lunch sent by Charlie's favorite deli, they discussed work related topics and Charlie liked the way Martha caught on to terminology fast. Widow of a man in the business upstate Wisconsin, Charlie had a good feeling. *Hmm. I had that feeling before, about Joanne. Way different time, younger woman with ambitious plans, the bitch.*

"Let's talk about salary, Martha."

"Joanne said you tend to be generous."

"Did she now? How presumptuous." At Martha's grimace, Charlie laughed. "I am generous. Be a Girl Scout. Honest, loyal and trustworthy and I'll never let you down. How's this figure?" She scribbled numbers on the back of an envelope like a car salesman and watched Martha's plucked eyebrows rise. "Fair yes?"

"Oh, yes. And thanks." Martha raised her hand in a three finger Girl Scout salute.

"Tomorrow eight a.m. 'til whenever. This summer I'm traveling back and forth to Fairview, Illinois, north of the city. When necessary I'll have my driver take you there. Okay?"

"Yes."

"This first week of orientation, I'll be here where we'll go steady. You'll meet my partner, my brother Jimmy and the rest of our associates including the CPA's next door."

"Roger that," Martha said. They closed up and rode down together, the beginning of a new association.

Chapter 16
Tom

Tom drove out to Haven, summer wind in his hair, a lot on his mind. Jerry refused to co-operate with wheel chair sports. There must be other sports for impaired people. Work at the law firm slowly improved. Corporations requested him to draw up contracts, annuities, tax exemptions, complex endowments a specialty. The interesting odd couple and oh so wealthy Anderson's in Fairview trusted him and began heading friends in his direction. His future grew brighter each passing day. He hoped to see Joanne McKenna Friedman at Haven and when he arrived, Charlie said she no longer worked for her. In fact, Charlie never even had a phone call and figured Joanne was too busy studying for Bar exams to call her old boss. From the look on Charlie's face, she was disgusted.

A storm was in the forecast but over the Great Lakes, one never knew. It could blow over or not. Meanwhile Tom knew that soon supermarket shelves would empty, no milk, water, staple items as locals prepared. Smug in the knowledge he'd done a quick shop the night before, made sure his folks were set and he had a full tank of gas. For a Saturday morning, the highway had few cars heading north instead of the usual bumper to bumper.

Haven lived up to its name. Peaceful with colorful sweet smelling flowers in bloom along the path. Unfamiliar with names, Tom gave up and enjoyed the sights and scents of a paradise Charlie created. Grateful he'd become friends with the brilliant girl who showed up at high school one morning to outrun and outshine all the other girls. She'd walked up the wide steps with her uncle, the prominent lawyer Stuart Alfred, head held high, auburn hair blazing in the summer sun. And he, captain of the football team, made it his business to watch over her in secret. Tom grinned at the memory. As if a smart girl didn't know he sent his teammates, one at a time, to protect her. And Charlie, tough and resilient, could take care of herself. *The only one she allowed close enough to hurt her was me.* Interesting how she liked playing 'remember when' each weekend he came up. As if the past seemed brighter than her present life.

Parking, Tom grabbed his gear and headed around the back before going in. Haven buzzed with activity and delicious aromas tempted him wafting through open windows. His nose twitched. Bacon, oh yes. And what else? Something in the oven or on the range. Ms. Jackson working her magic. Did the bundle of energy ever sleep? The cloudless blue sky showed no sign of a storm. Hmm. Just in case, he stowed his bag in the big outside locker, secured the handle and hurried in.

"Hey gang, is there a snitch or two of bacon left for a hungry man and maybe a leftover eggie?"

An array of small children giggled. Emma said, "The word is egg, Tom. Not eggie. That's for little kids." More giggles.

He pulled up a seat. "I'm a little kid. Just taller and if I want to say eggie, my mommy says it's okay."

Shelley messed up his blond hair. "Funny man. Never thought you'd have a way with kids." She passed a filled breakfast plate to him. "Are you here for Jerry?"

He nodded. "Maybe shooting basketballs in a lowered net and some dribbling maneuvers." A crisp piece of bacon disappeared in his mouth, teeth chomping all the way. "What do you think? Too strenuous?"

Shelley walked around the table wiping little mouths and hands and giving instructions to the kids. Jake and Luke, age four were in charge of their twin sisters, Dawn and Amelia age three. The boys were white, the sisters a luscious caramel color. The parents knew their combination of white and black heritage might produce different combinations and after a shaky beginning, they stopped worrying about it.

Tom admired Shelley's confidence and waited for an answer. When the kids were sorted out with activities, she sat next to him sipping iced tea already beads of condensation beginning to slide down the glass.

"I have an old net set up low enough for Jerry. Dribbling might be a prob, the turn at the waist, you know. On the other hand," she turned from her non-existent waist, "try it, watch carefully and see if it causes any pain. Anything active you get him to do will be appreciated. He's lost his will to try. Tom," she touched his arm, "I've done a lot of research and I'm working on a different path of ideas to help my friend. Maybe, if you keep an open mind, you can help. Between you and me, he doesn't want to improve. "

Shelley's Gram, quiet 'til now, began to hum her smoky voice rich with soul from singing with the choir back in Mobile, Alabama. "Do I smell Jambalaya, Ms. Jackson?"

"You surely do, Tom but not for you less you call me Gram or Jane."

Tom laughed. "My pleasure, Jane."

"Hmm. Not good 'nuff, Tom. Gram'll do or nary another."

Their laughter blended and Tom knew he'd joined the Haven family.

Jerry shielded his eyes against the bright sun. "What's with the forecast? So far so good." Sweat dripped off his tanned nose. He reached for another towel tucked into the side pocket of the wheelchair and dried off. "Humid, though."

"You never know when a storm might hit or when it rolls out over the lakes. Just like life."

Jerry threw the basketball hard as he could right at Tom's mid section. Air burst from Tom's lungs on impact and he fell hard to the court gasping. When he found his voice, he croaked, "What the hell? Why'd you do that?"

Jerry, a satisfied look on his face said, "I don't need a reminder of storms and life and accidents." He yelled at Tom. "I live with this, you jackass. I'm to blame. No one else. My fault I sit here learning to fucking toss a stupid ball in a hoop and dribble a basketball. Don't you get it?" He turned the wheelchair and rolled away without use of the motor.

God, the guy is strong not using the motor. Time for a consultation with Shelley. I hope he didn't break a rib. Man that hurt.

Holding his ribs, he loped toward Jerry calling out. "Sorry. I'm thoughtless, okay. I meant no harm. Please forgive me, Jerry."

The wheelchair slowed and stopped. Tom saw Jerry's shoulders shake, his head drop forward. *Geez! What to do?* Tom had a brother. He knew when someone cried. Especially a guy.

"Jer, you've got a mean right hook, ya, know? Good thing all you threw was a ball. Do you know anything about ribs?"

"Barbecue?"

"No, you damn fool. My ribs. One might be re-arranged or cracked. I can't tell. Hurts like hell."

"I have x ray vision eyes."

"No shit, Jerry. I'll ask Shelley. Don't worry. I'll say I tripped and fell."

"Big cover-up, Tom. Downtown we call it Jerry Kahn-Gate."

The wind picked up and the sky darkened. Excited voices inside Haven called out, "Lock the windows, toys inside, nor'easter's comin'."

The men hurried in and Shelley took one glance at Tom's middle, grabbed an ice pack, gave it to the wounded Tom muttering, "You men," and hurried for an elastic wrap.

Jerry said, "A band-aid will do, Shelley."

"All heart, my friend. I'm out of here."

Tom hung tight to the steering wheel all the way home, strong gusts of wind threatening to blow his car off the highway. Thoughts turned to Joanne. *I wonder why she's such a loner and why she hadn't called her once close friend Charlie in two weeks. Since we both live in Old Town and I've already scoped out her address not far from my place, I figure it won't hurt to stop by. And speaking of hurt, I'm in a world of hurt from the rib thing. No time for an accident. Not when life blooms for me.*

Joanne's little red convertible was parked where he'd seen it before.

No harm in ringing the bell to say hi. First floor apartment. No lights. Out on a date? Nah. Not if she studied for the bar exam. No power? Other apartments had lights. Worry crept into his thoughts as the wind howled. *A woman alone in danger.* He rang the bell. No answer. Knocked on the door. Still not a sound. Knocked harder and harder. Called her name loud. No answer. What if she was injured, couldn't call for help? Oh Geez. What to do? Pumped with fear he remembered Patrick's don't-leave-home-without-it card and removed the one credit card he owned, or it owned him, from his wallet. It worked just like on all the cop shows.

Small flashlight turned on, Tom scanned a small living room and sniffed stale air as if the windows had been closed for a while. "Joanne, you here? It's Tom Donnelly." A voice startled him.

"Don't move. I have a gun pointed at you."

What have I gotten into blundering in playing the good Samaritan and now the crazed woman has a gun? Time to talk her out of this madness.

"Whoa, Joanne. I come in peace. Charlie and I were worried about you. I live close by and it made sense for me to make sure you're okay." He stepped closer as he spoke, a tactical move practiced on the football field a million times.

"Shut up and get out. I'm uh, fine."

The hesitation in her voice urged him on. "I'm hungry. Have you eaten?" The apartment needed airing and no cooking smells were evident.

"What day is it?"

"Put the gun down, Joanne and we can talk while I cook." The flashlight caught sight of her, hands shaking when she placed the gun on the carpet. Gone was the poised, cold demeanor replaced by a sad, frightened woman.

"Tom Donnelly? It's you? Why? I'm a mess. I uh, took the Bar exam and got scared I didn't pass so I holed up here to uh, wait."

He crawled over next to her and sat. "You could wait a long time. Results don't come in so fast. Took me three times before I passed. Thought the firm would kick my sorry butt out. Hey, meanwhile, let's order something or I can whip up an omelet if you have eggies in the fridge. You like over-easy, poached, scrambled?" Distraction worked; her breathing slowed and she made eye contact.

"Canned chicken noodle soup and oyster crackers."

"Wow. My favorite." Inside he cringed missing Gram's Jambalaya for canned soup. "When did you take the exam?"

"Monday."

"Today's Saturday. You must be running on empty. How about a shower..." he felt her shrink away, "while I warm the soup." Rising clumsily, pain in the rib, Tom made it to the kitchen, fumbled for lights and found soup, crackers and a lot of fruit. Strawberries beginning to shrivel, blueberries, wilted salad, apples. He bit into a Gala apple, his favorite. Tasted great. "A nor'easter's about to hit. Do you want to let some cool air in before the rain?"

No reply. Down the narrow hall, he heard the shower turned on. He cranked open a few windows, watched shutters chatter from wind picking up. Fresh air felt good. As soon as the shower turned off, Tom closed the windows and warmed chicken noodle soup. *Ask Joanne if she has flashlights, batteries, candles, bottled water just in case power goes down.*

Hair dripping, Joanne wore baggy sweats, a towel around her neck. "Eggies?"

"Huh?"

"You said eggies." Lightning crackled followed by a thunder roll across the sky.

Tom recalled the word and chuckled. "Yeah. I had breakfast at Haven with the kids..."

"You had breakfast at Haven this morning?"

"Well, yes, I did. What's the big deal?"

"And Charlie was there?"

Tom held up his hands. "Joanne, she's there for the summer. It's Saturday. I've been going to Haven Saturday's to help with Jerry and the kids." He took a deep breath and rose to leave. "I don't get it, Joanne. I'm just ..."

She shouted. "You're just worming your way back into her life is what you're doing, Thomas Donnelly. I've known men just like you."

At the door, he spun around to face her. "You know nothing about me. Charlie and I were kids, seventeen when we loved each other for maybe a week. She was the first girl who said no to me. Me, the big man on campus and I couldn't take it. My life fell in the toilet and now I'm doing my damndest to be a friend. That's all. Case closed. Call me when you get over yourself. You need batteries, candles, water, food. Call." He slammed the door. "And get a better lock." He turned back. "And where's your doorman?"

"Attrition. They let him go. Damn."

Chapter 17
Joanne

It's not possible he's telling the truth. Men lie. I learned that much the hard way. Carefully Joanne wrung water from her hair and slowly brushed long strands 'til they dried. The wind picked up to rattle the windows. Get a better lock, Tom said. He also suggested a list of provisions in case the power went out. An inventory of the refrigerator proved she needed food and fast. Call, he said. Fat chance. *Rely on no one but yourself, lady. He took the exams three times before he passed. Is he dumb or a man at odds with himself. Who gives a shit. Not me.*

With her gun in the pocket of a light windbreaker, she locked up and ventured out in the empty street. Joanne rushed to the local store and found everything she needed, just in case. The grocer, Mr. Loman, was always pleased to see her with so many customers going to the supermarkets now. He offered a ride or to carry her bags but Joanne declined. Head down laden with bags, she sprinted two blocks to her apartment and entered the building just as the rain blew sideways and as predicted, power went out.

In the dark, she fumbled around finding what she needed and before long flashlights lit her way. A sense of accomplishment filled her. Once again, she took care of herself. A nagging thought: *with a little help from Tom Donnelly, don't forget.* A can of Sterno lit and soon warmed soup gone cold. *Delicious. Tom must have been thinking about Shelley's grandmother's homemade soup when all I have is canned. Hmm. I bet she makes Jambalaya.* Her mouth watered for a taste. *Tom said eggies. That's a funny word for a man to say. Of course when you're around those adorable kids, why not? Stop thinking about him. He's nothing to me.* Her cell phone rang.

Caller I.D. showed Tom Donnelly.

"How did you get this number?"

"Charlie gave it to me. She's worried about you, the storm. I don't care, of course. I'm calling for her," Tom said. And laughed.

Good thing he couldn't see the third finger she extended. "What?"

"Did you get to the store before the power blew?"

"Not your business."

"Call Charlie. She's worried. Haven has power."

"Good for her. You took the exam three times? Really?"

"Scout's honor. I'm holding up three finger salute. That's the total truth."

"Oh." She lit a candle and sat cross legged on the couch. "How come?"

"Nitwit. Screwed up priorities. I'm better now since January first. Resolutions and all."

"Okay. Tell Charlie I'm fine. Good night. And uh, thanks." Alone without the sound of Tom's voice she half smiled while the wind howled just the other side of the window. *So close. Too close.*

The power came back on the next morning bright, the calm after the storm, Joanne dressed for running. Church bells rang. She shut her ears to the sound. *This has nothing to do with me. Forced to go with mother and the older kids, I vowed never to step into a church again.* Slowing, she came to a synagogue and thought of Poppa, her only pal. *Once he brought me to his place of worship where the people spoke a different language he called Hebrew revealing a* side of him she'd never known; and became a secret they shared. The worst was that he traveled so much, died way young and couldn't protect his baby girl. Almost tempted to enter the old building, she hurried on and ran the distance to a health club.

In the small clean silent apartment she knew some changes had to be made. The law firm opened up possibilities of friends. After so many years of being a loner, shutting people out maybe... No Charlie and no Tom who really tried last night. She ran out to Mr. Loman's store to buy fresh basil, box of pasta, bottled sauce and six red roses for an early dinner celebration. Whoopee.

At her door, Joanne found a bouquet of red roses complete with baby's breath and fern in a glass vase. On the little white card an inscription read: *Here's to power on. May your day be as bright as you. Tom Donnelly.*

Damn the tears and damn him for provoking this reaction, she thought. I *have no room for anyone in my life.* Lifting the vase to inhale the scent, she knew these were not hot house roses like the six from the shop down the street. Fresh from somewhere special and thorn-less. Tom so thoughtful. Now she'd have to call and thank him and blah, blah, blah. The way real people do and then a friendship begins and NO she did not want a friend.

Inside, Joanne put everything on the counter and made the call hoping for voice mail.

"Hey Tom, the roses are," choked up she almost cried and stopped to clear her throat, "the roses are uh, special. Thanks. Bye."

"Joanne, don't run away. I was thinking about you, so I sent them to brighten up the table. No biggie."

"Okay. Gotta go."

"Wait a minute, wait a minute. Any plans for dinner?"

One glance at purchases made a short time ago; pasta in a box, sauce in a jar, fresh basil to sprinkle. Joanne the chef. "Early dinner of spaghetti. Nothing fancy after my day and I start a new job tomorrow."

"New job? With a law firm?"

"Yes. I'm excited about it. All my professors recommended me to this firm and after an interview, I was accepted. Speaks well for night school."

"Speaks well for you, Joanne. So do you want to have a real dinner out with me?"

The Catch

Real dinner? He's casting aspersions at my meal. Well two words for him and they're not Happy Birthday. "Thanks but no. I'll do my thing here. Alone. Thanks again for the flowers. They smell, hey what's a good word for the scent of fresh roses?"

He laughed. "Divine?"

"Divine. In my whole life, I never used such a word. Bye."

She inhaled the flowers again. The fragrance was divine. And Tom Donnelly was a man to stay far away from no matter how many flowers he sent.

Chapter 18

Wearing a gray pin striped suit, crisp white shirt cuffs peeking out of jacket, Joanne patted slicked back hair nestled into a knot at her neck and waited for the elevator. Six forty five a.m. A little early to give her time to adjust to new surroundings on the twentieth floor in this splendid building on Michigan Avenue. Packed in a slightly used, polished to a shine black leather case were lunch, sneakers, and a make-up bag. A crowd hurried in riding up, some quiet, others chatting and finally her floor where a few others walked out with Joanne.

At reception, she introduced herself to the attractive receptionist, charming so early in the day. "I'm Joanne McKenna Friedman.

"Welcome, Ms. Friedman. I'm Maggie Byron. L.B. will set you up in just a minute. Restrooms are there," she pointed right, "cafeteria to left. Good coffee."

Restless, Joanne waited for this L.B. person, her thoughts in a whirl expecting an old guy, employee with the company for years.

"Joanne?" a low male voice said her name.

"Yes, that's me." Joanne turned almost hitting a seriously handsome guy with her leather case.

"I'm L.B. Warren, your guide today. I'll show you the ropes, your space and explain what you will be doing at first. This is called the introduction to our firm. Follow me."

The Catch

A whirlwind day ended with Joanne rubbing aching feet to lace up sneakers and head to the elevator. On the way down, Tom Donnelly stepped in. They stared at each other.

"You work here?" They said in unison and laughed.

Outside in the warm July evening, Tom walked with Joanne. "What a surprise."

"I'll say. You never mentioned the name of your company."

"Neither did you."

They laughed again.

"Quick dinner?"

Oh why not, Joanne thought then shook her head. "No, thanks." *He's too dangerous.*

" Just when I guessed we might be friends you turn me down. Did my deodorant fail or what?"

Attempt at flippancy, never her strong point, failed. "Guess again." He appeared not to get it and hurt showed on his rugged face. "Tom, I don't trust anyone and I hold my feelings close. My job is what counts. You caught me at a weak moment the night of the storm. It's over, okay? I'm a survivor and from what you confided, you've got a way to go. Good luck and good bye."

Before he had a chance to respond Joanne vanished in the crowd.

In a cab he itched for the old life; stop for a drink or two during happy hour, pick up a pretty woman at the bar, be a good old boy. Eyes squeezed tight, he gave his address to the driver, told him not to stop even if he begged to get out. The cab driver swiveled his head around and nodded.

"You've heard this before?"

"Oh yeah. Ya think you're the only guy? Are ya married or just need a drink?"

"No to both. Just a damn fool." Tom wiped sweat from his brow and sat back to consider the next move. *Let her go. She has her agenda. I have mine.* He wanted a physical release with no romance in sight. In the past the old Tom, the catch, never needed to do the one hand mambo but maybe the time was ripe. He certainly was. The rib Jerry Kahn pounded a few days ago finally stopped hurting. Ergo, not broken. *Oh shit. Enough with introspection. Go for a run, make an eggie, spinach, cheese omelet and work on his best clients, the Anderson's, latest acquisition. Did I think eggie? Yes, I did. Joanne McKenna Friedman you've dug a hole in my heart. Damn.*

Chapter 19
Shelley

Uncomfortable, Shelley shifted position to elevate swollen feet. Gray hair curled around his white collar, the aging Doctor Cormack assured the anxious parents, the twins were doing fine. Jimmy exchanged a worried glance with Shelley.

"What about my darlin' wife? She's exhausted from these Braxton Hicks contractions. We packed a bag two weeks ago. Never leave home without it."

"Jim, I've taken care of Shelley for five years. She's a trooper. Call if there's any change, like contractions more frequent or prolonged in duration. Shelley, I know you won't listen but bed rest does help." He held up a hand before she could speak. "I know it's not your style but you're in the home stretch. Give all of you a chance."

"Uh, one more question." Shelley's cheeks burned. "Sex is okay?"

He rolled the little stool close and smiled. "Years ago we'd tell parents no sex eight weeks before delivery and eight weeks after. Then it was six weeks before and after. Times have changed. My feeling is sex can be a problem so gentle is the key word. Then you and the babies will be safe. We've got about two more weeks if you can hold on just like with the other deliveries and you all did fine. " After patting her hand, the doctor stood and left the room.

In medical school are doctors taught to pat patient's hands or squeeze a foot before they leave? I always wonder about dumb details. Sex. Hurray!

The Catch

In the peace of their sprawling ranch style home on the hill near Haven, kids and Gram asleep, Jimmy paced, his boots scuffing a trail through the carpet.

Dizzy watching her lanky husband, Shelly decided to stop him in his tracks. "Hey big boy, sit here," she moved on the wide denim covered couch making room and patted a place, "right close to me. Rest your head on my lap and feel the babies."

His warm body stirred the place in her core almost forgotten the past few months. Desire surged through her body. Swollen feet and belly forgotten, her woman's center blossomed waiting to open. She took his hand. "Jimmy, my love, press here."

Jimmy's blue eyes widened as his wife placed his hand between her legs. His voice grew husky. "Honey, is this wise? Once we start there's no going back."

She whispered in his ear. "Can't get enough of you, ever," And reaching down she felt his erection already throbbing.

Shelley raised eager hips and he slid cotton maternity panties down, not like the lacy ones she always wore to turn him on. It didn't seem to matter to her cowboy.

"Let's take this to the bedroom." Cupping her bare ass, Jimmy helped her stand. "Shh." Windows were cranked open to let night air and sounds pour in. Owls hooted a mysterious message across the woods, the nearby stream bubbled over boulders and an abundance of wild summer flowers perfumed the air.

Jimmy locked the door. The woman he loved shimmered in moonlight just like the first time they met at Haven, five years ago. She softened in their years together and he had grown up. They weathered a major storm when she didn't tell him about the first pregnancy and then she took a chance and told the truth.

Buttons of her dress were unclasped slowly He wanted to rip off the dress, to see her bare glistening chocolate skin. His wife was delicate now heavy with their babies. Careful, he thought. Her half smile taunted him. The dress fell to the floor.

God, how gorgeous and she was his. One girlish giggle and Jimmy shed his shirt, jeans, boots, and briefs fast as a firefighter when the bell rang. Arms around each other, they stepped over clothes to reach the extra long king size bed, just right for them.

"How's this gonna work, huh?"

With the wisdom of the ages and a few tips from sex books, Shelley sat at the edge of the bed. "How 'bout if I sit right here and you, darlin', would y'all mind kneelin' at my feet?"

"Sounds like a plan. But how 'bout some serious kissin' 'n foolin around first?"

"Oh, like foreplay?"

"Uh huh."

Kisses sweeter than wine. The old song ran through Jimmy's head when they began to kiss as if it were the first time. A touch of the lips, a taste, tongues danced and sucked in an intimate embrace. Licking vanilla scented skin all the way to Shelley's full breasts, Jimmy pulled gently on her dark taut nipples, a feast as he worked his way down patting the mound, feeling rolls of baby kicks then quiet when he reached her special place. His special place. His cock throbbing with nowhere to go just now, he squeezed it and parted her legs.

"Okay so far, baby?"

"Mmm."

He tasted her nectar and felt like a god. How delicious, a meal for a starving husband as he held open the lips and tasted, licked the sides and forced himself not to cum. Not yet. Not 'til she was satisfied. In and out went his tongue like a piston, slow and faster and he felt her insides begin to quiver and vibrate. Juices flowed, she held his head and cried out, "Oh, yes."

Tears coursed down her cheeks when Jimmy held her, his cock stiff, waiting. Finally she pressed close as possible and held the length of him in one hand. Reaching between her legs, she gathered slick juice to annoint him up and down.

"Feels good? You like?"

The Catch

With a laugh, he carefully straddled her chest. "Too heavy?"

"No, love. Let's give it a shot...or two." And they did.

Much later, they talked about Doctor Cormack's suggestion of bed rest and agreed Shelley would try.

Chapter 20

"Welcome to a quiet Haven for a pleasant change."

Shelley greeted her special client, Jerry Kahn, from a prone position on the couch in her office. "Doctor's orders. Get off my feet."

From his wheelchair, Jerry quipped. "That makes two of us."

"You haven't lost your droll sense of humor although it's taken a dark turn."

His eyes spoke of grief. *I need to reach him and today I'll use some ammunition.* "Let's start with a different concept." Jerry's closed his eyes and pretended to snore. "You're acting like Emma on a bad day. Listen or you'll be the loser." He caved. "Did any of your specialists in Chicago mention hysterical paralysis?"

Moments passed while she watched her good friend, brows furrowed, dig back to the post-accident care.

"No. Don't think so. So much going on. A confusing time."

"Okay. We'll move on. I've been researching spinal cord injury and came across an article about hysterical paralysis. Digging deeper, I found that loss of motor function," she gestured toward his legs, "can be precipitated by a traumatic event. The accident."

Surprised at his reaction, Shelley saw Jerry give a dismissive hand wave, spin the wheelchair fast, careening into the coffee table. His strong arms reached out preventing a crash. Righting his chair, Jerry gasped for breath. Mumbling curses Jerry propelled the motorized chair toward the door picking up speed again.

Acting as if her friend didn't just save himself from possible disaster, Shelley's voice bellowed. "Jerry, get the hell back here and pour us some ice tea. We have work to do."

A sheepish grin tugged at the corner of his mouth as he wheeled around to follow instructions. "You're scary when someone doesn't listen, Shelley Costigan."

"Damn straight." They clinked glasses, drank Gram's ever present tea. "Jer, you almost."

"So I did." He rubbed his head. "Shel, I really did save myself. The old reflexes kicked in fast." He held out his hands and examined them. "All the weights lifted to strengthen my arms worked."

"Yes. Speaking of strength, you pretty near broke at least one of Tom's ribs throwing a football at him not long ago. Why'd you do that?"

She held her breath watching as the mention of Tom brought a storm to Jerry's eyes. "I look at him and see a strong good looking guy, whole and capable of loving my wife the way he did back in the day. The opposite of me. I'm angry and... and hopeless. So I threw the football hard as I could. In retrospect, I'm sorry. It's not his fault. It's mine. I'll apologize when and if he returns."

"Point well taken. You've heard the expression, "Sorry for your loss?" Jerry nodded.

The wheelchair inched forward and they were almost eye to eye.

"Let's analyze your situation. You've sustained a loss because of the accident. Use of your legs. So you feel you're not a whole person anymore." Jerry nodded again. "Tom once loved Charlie, maybe for a week, Jer and they were teens. We're almost thirty now. He came here to lend a hand with his expertise, sports. Between us, I think he's interested in Charlie's former office manager."

"Joanne? Huh."

Shelley continued. "If there's a possibility for you to walk again, how hard would you try?"

She crossed her fingers to observe Jerry as his eyes searched a distant place exploring the idea.

"I'd give my left nut, Shel."

She couldn't stop a laugh from bubbling up. "That's the spirit. There's a process called functional electric stimulation, FES, to restore and or improve function of paralyzed muscles."

Attention captured, Jerry leaned forward. "This is not some mumbo jumbo crap. It's a proven technique?"

"From what I've read, yes. So there's hope and that's what we need here."

Shelley saw a tiny spark ignite in Jerry; shoulders straightened as his natural curious nature grabbed hold. "Tell me more."

Inside her mound babies rolled and pressure increased below. *Not now, not again, she thought.* Stifling a wince, Shelley continued. "If you decide to try FES, you'd have daily treatment for two weeks with current applied to your quadriceps in hopes of reversing paralysis of the anterior muscles."

Slumping back in his chair, Jerry sighed. "Happy student once at NU and look at me now. Almost too much to bear, Shel."

She patted her belly. "That makes two of us, Jer." Old friends shared a laugh. "I have literature about FES, a contact number, website and references we can look at together and you will want to discuss this with Charlie. It's not a new procedure. Been around since the seventies. Now before you race off to wrap your mind around this I'd like to discuss a few more topics of a personal nature. And please listen."

White knuckled hands held onto his wheelchair. Before he tried to disappear again, Shelley spoke, her voice one of authority. "Your wife believes you don't care about her anymore."

"What?" Color drained from his face.

"She confided in me. Charlie's so afraid of losing you, Jerry," Shelley took his cold hand in hers and he didn't pull away, "look around you. You're not the only one the accident affected. Think of your daughter. Emma's four and a half, smart and appears to be carefree but believe me, she's deeply disturbed by what's happened to her daddy and feels tension between you and her mommy."

"I never thought..."

"Of course you didn't. That's why we're talking. Communication is what life is all about."

"What can I do?" Glasses removed, he polished them.

Good, he wants answers and trusts me to help. "Someone wise once told me marriage is one long conversation. Jimmy and I follow that concept. And Jerry, we put a lot of lovin' into our marriage."

Tears turned to a sardonic laugh. "How the hell am I going to do that?"

"I always envied you and Charlie; your relationship and trust. Between the two of you, find a way to pleasure each other. You won't regret it.

The raucous sound of laughter broke the peace of Haven. "Mommy, mommy," high pitched voices called down the hall.

"Kids are back from camp. Let's talk later, okay?"

Jerry kissed his therapist on the forehead. "I have a lot to think about and work on. This might be a break through day. Thanks, Shelley."

Chapter 21
JoAnne

Joanne picked up the daily routine at the law firm with ease. Accustomed to the hectic pace at C. Stuart Construction followed by night school, she adjusted well. Lawyers were a different breed she discovered, intense, brooding, not all friendly, everyone with the plan for billable hours and financial gain. A couple of guys looked her over, offered after work refreshments. She always smiled, said no thanks and left alone to hurry back home The mail slot became a thing to be feared and prayed for. News regarding the Bar exam still hadn't shown up.

Maybe the envelope got lost in the mail, she wondered. Tom took the test three times before he passed. I'm smarter. The fucking test was so damn hard. With no one to whine to she paced the small room and worried. *Two weeks ago I thought maybe I aced the damn test and now I probably didn't pass. Shit.*

Almost knocking the nice mailman over, Joanne fumbled with the small key, breathed deeply to get a grip and opened the narrow box. *You've got mail, girl. Now let's see.* An official letter, Ms. Joanne McKenna Friedman. She dropped it to the tile floor in the entrance as if it contained anthrax. She stared. It didn't move. Her future lay on the floor and her hands shook so bad...

The old guy from upstairs opened the door. "You dropped a letter, Ms. Friedman." Stooped already from obvious scoliosis, he didn't have far to reach. "Here you are. Have a nice evening." And he handed her future over like he'd done a small courtesy.

"Thank you." Joanne's voice quavered. Locking the box, she opened her apartment door, closed and double locked to sit and stare some more. *Enough already, Poppa called from beyond the way he used to. Let's see what my smart little girl's accomplished today.* Okay Pops, here goes everything and out came the envelope opener to slide under the closure. And the answer is. .

Night wrapped Chicago in darkness. Stars came out to brighten the sky with a half moon shining. Wailing saxophones played jazz in the many clubs where tables filled to the streets in Old Town. In Joanne's dark apartment, she lay in bed still dressed, the letter clutched in her hands. *I did it, Poppa. Your little girl did it.*

She called Charlie.

"What? You dumped me like a hot potato, Joanne. What the hell happened? All you had to do was come straight with me. I trusted you, our friendship. Now what?"

"Please forgive me. I acted like a fool. I want to share my good news and I have no one to tell but you. I passed the Bar exam the first time."

"Well, good job. Joanne, if you need a friend you might consider being one. A good friend doesn't walk away to leave a friend in need. And Tom Donnelly would very much like to be your friend. He's been a big help at Haven and he's a good man. Someone I believe you can trust. Now it's late. Good luck and take care."

Hmm. I deserved that. Will the real lawyer stand up, she thought and laughed. Time for a bite to eat and get ready for tomorrow.

Busy at her desk the next morning, Joanne didn't quite hear the hint of excitement in L.B.'s voice when he entered her, not spacious to call anything but a cubby hole, personal space.

"Mr. Bancroft requests your presence now."

"Who?"

"Hugh Bancroft of Bancroft Law and Associates, you idiot. Hurry."

Rising in haste, Joanne dropped pens, papers and files on the floor; stooped to gather them but L.B. hustled her out the glass doors to the elevator and pushed the up button. "You're headed to the top in this firm, Joanne. Congratulations."

"You've heard?"

"News travels fast."

Elevator doors opened to the penthouse where a suite of rooms with mahogany carved doors stayed closed. Luxurious beige pile carpet wall to wall helped create a hushed atmosphere. Oil portraits of elder statesmen, founders of the firm with Bancroft as the last name, hung along one wall. An elegant woman right out of Vogue, sat at a carved wormwood desk, her platinum hair swept back in a chignon, make-up perfect. Dressed in an off- white silk shirt, ruffled down the front exposed enough to display cleavage and a designer suit in black caused Joanne to feel tacky. Her clothes were bought from a specialty shop where wealthy women wore them once never to wear again. *I am so out of place here.* A small brass sign placed on the middle front of the magnificent desk indicated her name: Tina Endicott.

"Ms. Friedman," a cultured voice matched the elegant woman, "Mr. Bancroft will see you now. L.B., thank you for escorting Ms. Friedman. That will be all."

Dismissed, L.B. stepped close to Joanne and whispered, "You'll be great. Take mental notes and tell me later."

I won't, she thought and followed Ms. Endicott to Mr. Bancroft's office. *I've got to find out what perfume she uses. Wow!*

To Joanne's surprise, Hugh Bancroft appeared to be a kindly gentleman with snow white hair and a paunch. Like Santa Claus; if Santa ran a multi-million dollar corporation and had the reputation of a take-no-prisoners capo de tutti capo without being Mafia. She shook in her high heels and tried to control herself.

"Well, well. My instincts were on target when I first read reports about you, Ms. Friedman. Of course, with all my experience and the partner's comments, and the fact you came highly recommended. Now this." He held up an envelope similar to the one she received yesterday. "You passed the Bar exam the first time." A smile creased his face briefly and he became all business.

"We expect great things from you. George Arnold, one of our exceptional lawyers, has a case he wants you to sit in on today at noon. This will get your feet wet, so to speak. Congratulations. A bonus is forthcoming immediately. The instructions will be left at your desk. I think," rubbing his chin, "I think we'll move you to a different space today. L.B. will know." He extended his manicured hand, soft and supple as kidskin and they shook hands.

Almost stumbling on her way to the door, Joanne realized she never uttered one word the whole time. Santa did all the talking. *Let me get through this day. I'm getting a bonus and an opportunity to sit in on a case. Did he mean court case? Of course he did. Joanne McKenna Friedman, you're on your way.*

In the short elevator ride down from the inner sanctum, Joanne pinched herself back into reality. *This is what I've dreamed of, worked for. It's here and all I have to do is focus and prove I'm valuable to Bancroft.*

L.B. showed his handsome face over the top of the cubicle and grinned. "Pack up. I have orders from on high to relocate our brightest star." Feeling hostility from everyone, Joanne packed and moved down the hall to a small office complete with a desk couple of chairs, and a window. She glanced out and did a double-take. Just a peek of the tiniest corner in sight of Lake Michigan, but hers to hear and if she squinted, to catch a glimpse.

L.B.'s deep voice interrupted her thoughts. "I've been here a long time and never heard of anyone getting an office so soon. You'll go far at Bancroft. Put in the hours and work and you won't regret it. Now have a snack and spiff up. George Arnold's sending orders shortly."

He's been here a long time? L.B. looked young, about twenty something. Today when he moved close I noticed crow's feet around his eyes, creases near his mouth. Maybe he was closer to forty and so nice. What job did he hold at Bancroft? she wondered.

Joanne took a moment to focus on the task ahead. First she unpacked a few personal items; pens and stuff, checked for a key to lock her bag in the desk, happy to find two on a ring. Next she ate a granola bar, drank a bottle of white grape juice and make-up bag in hand, strode to the restroom to 'spiff up' in L.B.'s words. Thankful with no one around, Joanne applied concealer on the scars and refreshed her makeup, careful to brush her teeth removing all trace of crumbs. Fresh lipstick, a re-comb of hair smoothed back into a sleek knot at her neck and she examined herself in the long mirror.

Did she look too severe? Nah. Strictly business is the way she liked it. Later she'd go for a softer look. Satisfied, Joanne hurried back to the office; her office, to try out the new chair and wait for the day to open like a gift.

Crossing wide Michigan Avenue in high heels was definitely a challenge and trying to keep up with long legged George Arnold who strode full steam ahead...almost impossible. Paul McCann, freckles, red hair and a bit stocky for a youngish guy, was Mr. Arnold's first assistant. He grabbed Joanne's arm and helped steer her.

"Thanks, Paul. Next time I'll wear sneakers and race you across to the courthouse." Joanne carried two brief cases, Paul had a stuffed litigation bag while the head lawyer talked on a cell phone, arms free. "Are we his lackey's today, Paul?"

"Oh yeah, and proud of it. Today's case is complex. The wealthy woman says her lover stole jewelry before breaking up. Mr. Arnold intends to prove her case although there is no real proof. He said, she said. Arnold is good as you'll find out. Watch, listen, take notes. This is a great opportunity for you." He squeezed her arm. "A drink after work?"

Uh oh. A come-on from another lawyer more established. "Thanks, Paul. I like to get home and relax. Early to eat and get to sleep." Smiling up at him she hoped he'd understand no offense meant. "I appreciate your advice. Definitely I need all the help you can give."

They hurried up the steps into the impressive Hall of Justice. Joanne's breath caught at the familiar statue with balanced scales. A bundle of excitement surrounded her as they rode the crowded elevator and strode toward the courtroom. Lawyer Arnold, dressed in a navy blue suit, power red tie knotted to perfection, swaggered as he entered, shaking hands, waving to others. Joanne watched every movement picturing herself, elegant and assured without showing off. *Give me a year or two and I'll be trying a case.*

Paul led her to the table where they spread out clean yellow legal pads, laptops and readied themselves for what came next. Joanne read through files Paul had sent earlier. She found two flaws and didn't have time to research precedents before being called to meet them downstairs. Fresh from law school, she'd stored a lot of information in her memory bank and had tons of notes in files. She may not help Mr. Arnold but he probably didn't need any. With an inward sigh, she sat up straight and concentrated, flipping page after page until an ah hah moment happened.

If her lover claimed he knew nothing about a diamond necklace how come he described it in great detail? It seemed like a stupid idea yet she searched the file and found no reference to it. Hmm. Delving further she found information about the lover's past relationships. Other women, all wealthy, were dumped by him after a hot six months or more. There were no complaints and no indication George Arnold spoke to them. About anything. What the hell? Puzzled she turned to Paul and stopped. The expression on his face clearly showed worship of his mentor. *Keep it to yourself.* She couldn't do it. During the course of the afternoon, she'd see how her information might be passed to the lawyer in charge.

During cross examination, the lover, Jonathan St. James, an extraordinarily attractive man-a Cary Grant look-alike who wore an ascot and spoke with an English accent, was asked by Counselor Arnold, "And the missing diamond necklace, did you ever see it, touch it to fasten around Mrs. Kaye's neck?"

"Of course not. The clasp was broken."

"You have testified you knew nothing of this necklace. Now you say the clasp was broken."

"I meant Mrs. Kaye told me about the broken clasp."

Absorbed in his technique, she watched as Mr.Arnold attempted to extract some damning information like something to pin on St. James. But the man was unflappable. Poised and assured of himself, he had Bancroft's finest stymied.

"Nothing further, your Honor."

Returning to our table, the chief's mouth set in a tight thin line. Joanne had written notes with questions about past relationships with wealthy women. 1.Maybe one of them missed jewelry after he'd gone. 2.Question mark after life style. 3.Life style improvement after jewelry gone missing? 4.Somehow get him to describe this necklace he claims he's never seen. Joanne had Paul check her notes. He gave the okay and she passed them to Mr. Arnold. He glanced, did a double take, scratched the stubble already growing back on his chin and asked for an audience with the judge. Both lawyers approached the bench; Joanne imagined a lot of hushed lawyer speak going on for a couple of minutes. Meanwhile Paul and Joanne were to investigate. Fast. The afternoon had come to a close. The judge pounded the gavel and left the chamber. Reconvene tomorrow at ten a.m.

All plans for an early dinner and sleep faded. They went to the law library, coffee and croissants in hand and researched, made calls and by ten slapped high fives with good progress. After tracking down several widows, each of whom hung up on Joanne when she mentioned the name St. James, she finally hit pay dirt. A woman of means, Elizabeth Walsh, agreed to testify that after a whirlwind romance, Jonathan St. James broke her heart and stopped calling. She discovered several valuable pieces of jewelry were missing soon after and too embarrassed and oh so wealthy, she let it go. Jonathan, it turned out, was not really a saint. Joanne offered transportation to the court house but Mrs. Walsh said her limousine would suffice and thanked her. She also said she looked forward to meeting the lawyer who finally gave her the guts needed to pursue the son-of-a bitch.

Paul complimented Joanne on her research, asked again if she'd like a drink, dinner, something as they rode down the elevator and walked to the curb. "As friends. Okay? I'm not asking to move in."

She found the energy to laugh. "Very cute. Thanks, Paul, not tonight." A taxi pulled up, she got in and was off to Old Town, her apartment and sleep. Body aching, she reached her door to find roses. A dozen red, divine as Tom called them, thorn-less and fresh. *Oh Tom. You know the way to my heart and I don't want you in here.* She slept fully dressed too exhausted to even kick off her shoes. Sometime in the night,

The Catch

Joanne awoke, stripped, drank water, and fell asleep again with red roses perfuming the small bedroom.

Chapter 22

Joanne opened the envelope and stared. Ten thousand dollars, the bonus check from Bancroft. She spun around and around in the black leather chair clutching the check. Her mind reeled with thoughts. *A wardrobe never worn by anyone but me; a real hairstyle and beautiful nails. Oh, stuff like rent and food and...*Another spin. Paul rapped his knuckles on the door.

"Nine o'clock. Let's go. Got a power bar and juice?"

"Thanks, Paul." She rose, gathered her briefcase, showed off clean sneakers. "Like the ensemble?" Today, she wore a light gray suit with a periwinkle blue tailored blouse, and pearl stud earrings. The outfit looked pretty but not exciting. *Wait 'til she went shopping, Bancroft. Then eyes would pop.*

"You look just about perfect. We did some amazing research last night. Actually you did, finding Ms. Walsh and convincing her to testify against St. James." He grinned. "I'll be carrying your bag in a couple of years. Damn, you're smart and fast."

"Flattery will get you everywhere." They headed out.

The elevator doors opened, Joanne stepped in and faced Tom. It wasn't unusual to meet working in the same building for the same law firm yet a surge of excitement rushed through Joanne. He'd transformed since the last time they met. Gone was the surfer look. Tom's dark blue suit draped just right over those broad shoulders. The blue shirt matched his eyes and the cuffs shot just enough at his strong wrists. *I'm checking out Tom like we're at a bar instead of a crowded elevator and I'm on my way to court.*

"We've got to stop meeting like this." Tom gave half a smile and turned her around to face forward. "Say goodbye, Paul."

The elevator door closed before Joanne knew what happened.

"I smell red roses."

Flustered, Joanne glanced back. Tom had jockeyed his way next to her. "Thanks. Roses are so beautiful, especially yours. I worked late and couldn't call to thank you but I was too tired."

"Next time. Good luck today." He left at the next floor.

Good luck? Word spreads even in a big law firm and apparently there aren't any secrets. By the time Joanne reached the lobby, Paul was there checking his watch. They hurried across the wide avenue. Her excitement grew with every step. *What will the chief Honcho do with the new information fed to him by my research?*

Smug and slick in an expensive Armani pin stripe, red power tie again perfect, *his lucky tie, I guessed,* George Arnold opened his mouth to speak when suddenly the doors flew open. An attractive mature woman decked out in elaborate jewelry, cane in hand, limped toward Jonathan St. James. Arms open wide, she said, "Johnny-boy, come back. All is forgiven. Mommy still loves you."

Mommy? What the hell. Who is she? I flipped through notes, found pictures copied from research of his former lovers and there she was. Mrs. Elizabeth Walsh. The wealthy widow who told me I gave her the guts needed to pursue the son-of-a-bitch. Now what happens?

Caroline Kaye, the plaintiff, grabbed Johnny-boy, the defendant, by one arm while Mrs. Walsh dropped her cane to grab the other arm. Joanne almost laughed with a picture they made: *Like a wishbone. Sad yet funny.*

Jonathan St. James smiled benevolently down at his ladies. He whispered in their sparkled-by-diamond ears. They nodded, sweet glances exchanged all around. Mrs. Kaye beckoned to George and spoke loud enough for words to float across to anyone within range.

"Drop the case, honey. Send me the bill. We're out of here."

The trio limped and marched out before the judge arrived.

"What just happened?"

Paul gathered our files and packed them into the two brief cases. "You've heard the expression 'case closed'?" Joanne blinked. "Well, the case just closed. Bancroft still gets the fee. If ever Elizabeth Walsh needs your services, get a retainer first. She'll remember you, Joanne. You're good. In fact when Bancroft hired you, the grapevine called you 'a catch'."

"A catch? I thought the word referred to a guy. Why me? That makes me feel like a fish on a hook."

"Get over it, Joanne. You've worked hard and it paid off. You're here among the top lawyers in Chicago."

How cool is this? The need to share the experience in court burned all day. "Who can I turn to when nobody wants me?" The old song ran through her mind all day. *Tom wants me but I can't let him in not even for conversation because one thing leads to another. Remember the terrible time...Don't go there.*

After work, Joanne hurried to a yoga class. She sought peace and hoped to lose herself there.

Chapter 23

Voice mail alert. Joanne listened as she stripped off damp yoga clothes. The weight of a stressful week lifted hearing Tom's voice.

"Your friendly flower delivery man calling. I'm going up to Haven tomorrow. Need company, preferably yours. I'm concerned about Jerry Kahn..." The message cutoff.

Hmm. He said friendly. I'd like a casual friend, a pal. Haven would be a change after hot humid Chicago in summer. So why not take him up?

She called him. "Tom, thanks. What time did you have in mind and can we go to the beach?"

"Who is this?"

Joanne took a deep breath, said nothing, and almost clicked off.

"Just kidding. I'm uh, happy that's all and I'll order a picnic basket for the beach and I have bug spray. Horse flies are vicious. Haven't been to the beach all summer. Nine o'clock okay?"

"After getting up at 4:30 every day, nine is like almost lunch break."

"Life of a lawyer. See you tomorrow."

Yeah, I'm definitely happy. For the first time in years I have more than a spark of happiness. With no one around to hug, Joanne hugged herself. Now where oh where was her swim suit?

The Catch

Buried at the bottom of the underwear drawer, she dug out her one and only suit; an old fashioned style that covered skin meant to be shown off according to fashion. *This won't do,* she thought. Dressed in shorts and a tee shirt, Joanne tied new sneakers fast and raced out the door to the shops nearby recalling a corner store with manikins in bikinis, sun hats and beach towels two blocks east.

Breathless, Joanne entered to glance around at the plethora of merchandise. Mystified as to where to begin, she froze. A perky salesgirl hurried over.

"You need help?"

"Oh, yes. I'm looking for a swim suit, please."

"Size?"

"Beats me. Uh, maybe a small."

Together they pulled a few off the shelf and Joanne was led to a small dressing room. Red with a ruffled bottom and a row of ruffles across the skimpy top. She tried it on and gasped. An invitation to get laid is what it looked like. Half her butt showed and tits...well, bend over to straighten the beach towel and they'd hang out. Uh, NO.

Only one fit just right with body parts covered enough and it sparkled with tiny silver stars on a royal blue background. Adding a white cover-up and flip-flops with a blue flower plus a white floppy sun hat, she paid and almost skipped to her apartment. With purchases spread out on her single bed and tags cut off, Joanne sang, "I Feel Pretty" from West Side Story and packed a small bag. She had a date.

Chapter 24
Nine a.m

Tom pulled up to the curb of Joanne's apartment building to find her leaning against one of the many old fashioned lamp posts that dotted Old Town streets. Gone the tailored lawyer and in her place, a carefree woman so pretty wearing a sun hat, shorts and shirt and spotless sneakers. *My date for the day. How lucky can I get,* he thought.

"Hop in."

Carry bag placed on the back seat next to a picnic basket, Joanne buckled in and they were off.

The hour of travel passed quickly as they swapped law talk and when she described the case of the jilted women and the hot lover with the abrupt finish, Tom laughed so hard, he had to pull over. Joanne told him to lift his arms above his head and then she pounded his back.

"Better?"

"I'll feel better when you stop pounding."

That set off more laughter so they opened the cooler in back and swigged water from dripping bottles before driving on.

The air changed as they got close to Lake Michigan. "Hear the sound?" Tom pulled up and stopped a few blocks before the beach. "This is a big bad lake. Most lakes lap at the shoreline. This one has boulders piled up and the waves often crash against them especially when the wind is up."

'Have you lived in Chicago all your life?"

"Yeah. Close to the city." He grinned and turned to Joanne. "How about you?"

"No. I kind of adopted this city. So far it's been very good to me. Mostly."

"Well, I hate to leave the beach area so let's come back in an hour after I check on Jerry."

He pulled his shirt up to show Joanne the faded bruise across his ribs still yellow and purple. "Jerry threw a football at me as hard as he could. Nearly broke a rib."

"Why would he do that?"

"A good question. Complicated answer, I guess."

Driving up the private road to Haven, Tom reached for Joanne's hand much smaller than his. "This is great fun and we're not there yet. Here's to a special day, as friends." He gently patted her hand. She squeezed his big hand.

"Friends."

Shelley

Shelley and Jerry made their way up a curvy path after early therapy. No one around with the kids on an excursion to a petting zoo, Charlie at work in the city and Jimmy at the new project. Quiet with only cicadas and chirping birds to break the silence and of course, the constant whirr of Jerry's wheelchair scooting ahead with Shelley plodding after.

She stopped, cried out with a stabbing back ache and suddenly a gush of water splashed between her legs. Knees buckling, she tried to break the fall but landed on her back half on the grass, half on the path. "Jerry, help." He moved on. Summoning all her strength she yelled. "Jerry."

The wheel chair spun around, rolled toward her. "Shelley, what happened?"

"Water broke. Call 911. Hurry."

Hands shaking, Jerry punched the numbers and listened. Nothing. No service bars visible.

"Shelley, there isn't cell phone service up here. What can we do?"

She cried out then panted as the pain subsided. Looked at her watch. "I'm having babies. The rest is up to you, Jerry Kahn. Do you have extra water bottles, towels in those big side pockets?" Another wave of pain rose, crested and fell. Labor in all its fury. She called. "Wipes-- alcohol wipes. I know you have some."

Fumbling in the side pockets, he found newspapers, water, clean towels and wipes and wrapped them in a tight bundle.

"Yes, I've got supplies but I can't get to you. Shel, I'm crippled."

"No you aren't. Crawl if you have to but you're gonna deliver my babies. Now get the fuck over here now. First put on the brakes."

He did as told, cringed as she moaned again remembering Charlie's labor four years ago. Using his arms, Jerry forced himself forward in the chair, used sense memory from therapy for leg motion and hanging one hand on to the arm of the wheelchair he lifted one leg and then the other to the path. He almost knocked himself out doing it and survived. Now he crawled dragging his legs behind toward Shelley, where blood began to trickle between her legs.

Joanne

Tom knocked on Haven's heavy door. He tried the door and found it unlocked. "Hello, anyone home?" No answer. "Maybe they're up on the path." They left the picnic basket in the kitchen. "Race you?"

"Watch it, I'm fast."

They ran laughing until Tom stopped. "Did you hear that?"

"It sounds like a commotion up ahead."

Jerry caught sight of Tom and waved. "Hurry. Shelley's in labor. Her water broke. She's in a lot of pain. Labor pain."

"What can I do?"

"Run back to Haven. Call 911 and get an ambulance." Tom ran.

Joanne moved in close and opened the switchblade she always carried. "Let me help. I have experience. Shelley, I'm going to cut your shorts to take a look, okay?" Shelley nodded and the knife cut right through shorts and soaked panties exposing a small reddish crown of hair."Shelley, you're crowning. Push. Breathe and push. Jerry, wipes or water for my hands fast." Jerry crawled forward with wipes.

Tom returned. "Ambulance on the way."

"Tom, pull out my shoelaces, quick." He did.

"You're good, girl. So good. I've got the head and here come shoulders. Oh, wide shoulders. A jock is on the way so breathe and push."

Focused on her job, Joanne still was aware of Tom watching the miracle before them. He'd never seen a birth before, a first timer mesmerized as she'd been long ago. Joanne caught the baby, curled and dripping with vernix, a whitish, cheesy stuff, eyes puffy. She worked as if she was an octopus. Her small hands were efficient, quick and always in motion.

"Shelley, congratulations. She's a red haired doll. You're a pro."

"Thank God and you, Joanne. And..." She groaned as another wave of pain gripped and squeezed. Contractions one after the other.

"Jerry, are you able to pass a water bottle over to me and a clean towel. And wipes. Fast."

"Here." Jerry tried to reach her but couldn't and Tom took over. "Open the bottle and we'll gently wash her and wrap her up." She glanced up, saw Tom and smiled. "This is the day at the beach, huh?" Cradling the baby, Joanne balanced the tiny body, cleaned out her mouth and rinsed and patted her dry. "Shoelace." Tom handed it to her. Tying it around the umbilical cord first, wiping the knife thoroughly with an alcohol wipe, Joanne made a quick cut of the cord, tied it and she placed her on Shelley's stomach.

"Oh, I forgot about a brother or sister. Sorry, baby." Joanne went into high gear. She lifted and wrapped baby one in a clean towel before handing her to Tom with a command for him to sit.

One handed, Tom loosened the jacket around his waist and sheltered the baby as he sat on a flat boulder.

"Shelley, wait just a darn minute, looks like we need a few more huffs and puffs because here comes the second one, push, breathe and push, Shelley, don't fade out on us. You're the expert." The twin arrived literally on the heels of the other. Not identical twins this time. "A brother with dark hair, Shel." He let out a yowl as soon as Joanne cleared his mouth. "Listen to him. He's happy to be here." The little girl had needed a bit of attention before she protested. Again Joanne cleaned the knife with wipes Jerry used for cuts and bruises and expertly repeated the process with the cord. She cleansed and wrapped the infant boy handing him to an exhausted Shelley and retrieved the sister from Tom. Shelley fastened one to each breast.

Sirens came closer. Shelley whispered, "Thanks Jerry. I knew you'd rise to the occasion. Wait 'til Charlie hears about this, Uncle Jer."

Jerry held her hand. "It's not my fault, Shelley. I believe it. You were right about everything." She nodded and turned to Joanne.

"What a woman you turned out to be. We couldn't have managed without you. And Tom, so fast on your feet, the ambulance will take over. Hey, call Jimmy please asap."

With some help from Tom, Jerry eased back in his chair to examine his cuts and scrapes. "Not bad for a handicapped person.

"Who's handicapped around here?" They both shrugged.

Joanne spoke to the EMS people recounting what she'd done without proper tools and antiseptics. "I hope they'll all be fine. I, uh, did the best I could under the circumstances."

Shelley said, "Gram always warned me about droppin' babies in the field and going on to finish pickin' cotton."

The ambulance doors shut, siren wailed, Joanne sagged against a tree. Tom cleaned up the area and the three of them went back down the hill.

The Catch

Jerry disappeared into his room saying he needed a shower and yes he needed a little bit of help so Tom did as asked. Joanne admired his willingness to be of service.

When he returned to the kitchen, he and Joanne stared at each other in disbelief.

"A day at the beach with a short visit at Haven?" Joanne cracked up. "You sure know how to treat a woman, Tom."

"Okay. So it wasn't exactly perfect."

"Oh yes. How perfect to deliver twins on a hillside with makeshift everything. I'll never forget this day, Tom. Now let's go to the beach after you make the calls and I wash up. Wait. I'm hungry. Can we picnic right here in the kitchen?"

"Sure." He called Jimmy who let out a yee haw.

"What about Shelley? Is she fine and the babies, what do we have now?" Tom heard a truck start up and knew Jimmy was on the way. "She's fine and you have a son and a daughter this time."

"And Dr. Cormack checked every one out. He's great. You met him, right?"

"Jimmy, Shelley will tell you about the whole experience. Uh, it's been quite an adventure. Gotta go. Congratulations. Oh, call Charlie. Jerry wants to talk to her."

He had some thinking to do as he laid out the tasty spread the best deli in Old Town had prepared for his date. *Joanne is someone special. Each time we're together: in an elevator, a phone call, the roses and today, I'm falling more in love with her. Be patient and hope she'll feel the same way before too long.*

Over towering lean corned beef sandwiches on rye with potato salad, and a little coleslaw, Tom finally asked the question de jour. "How did you know what to do? Or where did you learn how? Let me rephrase the question."

"Always the lawyer, Tom. Am I on trial or is this a getting to know me?"

He wiped a spot of mustard from the corner of her mouth.

"Thanks." She liked the intimate gesture. Liked it a lot.

"Call it getting to know more about you, Joanne. Is it too personal or can you reveal the source of your gift?"

Licking her finger, she picked up crumbs from the paper plate. "Mother was a mid-wife. Since I was the youngest child, she couldn't leave me home alone when she was called for a birthing so I tagged along. She demanded I be her maid; like second in command. No one knew I was under age, just eleven, when I watched and helped and by the time I was twelve, I'd delivered five babies." She looked around the table, her face no longer bright. "Are there any cookies?"

Tom moved around the table and put his arms around her. Rigid at first, Joanne relaxed against him. "Thanks for telling me. And I'm sorry you've had a bad time in your past. Maybe we can have fun together, as friends with no pressure, and put light in your life. What a day so far, huh? You brought twins into the world and I was a part of it." He lifted her chin. "I'll never forget today, Joanne. A toast?"

Tom peered into the fridge. "Gram's famous iced tea?"

"Yes."

Tom poured two glasses; they clinked and together said, "To today."

Chapter 25

Joanne changed into her new bikini swimsuit, to make sure no butt hung out in the back, and wished the top covered more flesh and gave up. *Burn marks don't show as far as I can see.* She slipped the cover-up over her head, pulled on the sun hat. *Flip flops felt good after being in sneaks all morning. I need new shoelaces. It was a good thing they were clean. Now Stop procrastinating and go to the beach.*

"Ready." She sailed past Tom and out the door, buckled up in the car before he'd said a word. The capable woman who delivered twins an hour ago was scared to death of disrobing at a beach.

"I guess you're in a hurry, Ms. Friedman. You forgot your beach bag."

He handed over the canvas tote, stowed a small ice chest on the back seat and away they went. A block away, Joanne laughed. "Listen. Your big bad Lake Michigan is calling." The private beach had an attendant who asked for I.D. Tom said, "Haven." A magic word there because they drove right in and parked in the one shady space over in a corner of the lot. At Tom's request she'd pocketed two beach passes from the kitchen in case anyone patrolling asked and Tom grabbed two towels, the ice chest and followed Joanne as she hurried toward the shore.

They agreed on a quiet section of sand away from families and spread out his towels. Joanne laughed at the wild print of hula girls, palm trees, and tigers. "Hey, don't laugh at my brother's towels."

"Why not? He's not here to defend himself."

"Pat's engaged. He figured she wouldn't like the print so I inherited them." He stripped off his shirt, six pack abs clearly defined. Swim trunks hugged a tight ass.

Joanne looked the other way, shaken to her core by this beautiful man, her date for the day, a friend. Uh huh. Sitting, she slipped the cover-up off one shoulder, shimmied down from the other shoulder and wriggled free. Undressing the hard way. Joanne shut her eyes and luxuriated in the heat.

"Sun screen, anyone? A walk along the shore first, get our feet wet. The lake is always chilly."

I know what he's doing. In the sweetest way, he's breaking down my reserve. Imagine that. Tom, a nice guy doing his best changing my former opinion for good.

"Sunscreen and a walk."

Joanne shivered at his touch when he squeezed lotion from the bottle and rubbed some on her arm.

"Thanks. I'm not used to anyone uh...helping. I'll get the rest." Averting her eyes from the hunk watching, she applied a quick splash of lotion. "Want me to uh do your back?"

"Sure."

Never do this with him again. A day at the beach seemed so innocent and now I'm orgiastic applying damn lotion on his spectacular shoulders and back and... "All set." She ran for her sanity, feet kicking up sand and reached the shoreline before Tom. "The water's warm."

"Here at the shoreline. When we go deeper, you'll find out how cold the lake is even on the hottest days."

"Deeper? I don't think so."

"Oh yeah. I rented a raft so we can paddle around."

Hmm. He's a man with a plan.

They walked along the shore away from families 'til they came to the boulders.

"Oh, look at that." She touched the jetty made of huge smooth boulders worn flat.

"Yup. Joanne, did you ever make sand castles with your thumb?"

"Nope. I bet you're going to show me."

Grabbing her hand, he pulled Joanne down to sit on the damp sand. "Hope you don't mind getting your swimsuit wet. It's so uh, pretty with all the little stars."

"I think it's meant to get wet, Tom."

"Okay. Move close to the shore and I'll make your first sand castle. Free. You can move right in."

She sat back admiring the way Tom's strong fingers dug a hole and the lake filled it. Using his thumb, he scooped wet sand and kept drizzling the funny little marbles he formed until a small castle grew. He grinned, white teeth sparkling. Guiding Joanne's hand, his on top, they added to the mound. Pressure on her thumb by Tom, she pushed in to the wet sand and working thumb and forefinger together little marbles dropped creating a taller castle. And she became aroused with all the push and rub, the sexual imagery; Tom on top. She could hardly catch a breath, a need to escape overwhelming her.

She rose and ran, plunging into the cold lake, the breast stroke, her strongest carried her far with nothing in view except blue sky and gray water until Tom caught up. They raced, matching stroke for stroke swimming beyond the limit when a lifeguard blew a warning whistle. Then they tread water to rest.

"Hey, You're fast."

"It's like riding a bike. You never forget but damn, it's freezing." She choked on small waves threatening to build, flipped around and headed to the beach and their little spot of sandy real estate for a few hours.

"Wow. I haven't done that since I was a kid. Hey, let's dry off, have a snack and sun a while." Joanne pulled the cover-up over her head and down. "Better. I hope Jerry's okay. You think he took a few steps?"

"Don't know. Be a miracle if he did." Tom shook his soaked blond hair in her direction and toweled off.

"Not fair." Joanne did the same with her wet long dark hair hitting his chin. "Gotcha."

The Catch

They played like kids snapping towels at each other and laughing. He picked her up and spun her around. "Are we having fun, or what?"

"Oh yeah. This is the best, Tom." *For just a little while I forgot my past. What a relief to be normal.* "Snacks." Without thinking, she pulled off her cover-up and sat cross legged while Tom cut crispy apples and sliced chunks of cheese on paper plates. Every morsel had grains of sand sprinkled on like beach crunch. On a one-of-a-day like this, who cared? Knees touching, aware of the contact, Joanne had an inner stirring. Tom stretched out and patted the space next to him.

"Relax. Enjoy the breeze."

Bodies close, silence hung between them like a sensual curtain as sounds of families nearby faded away and they were the only ones alone on this small private beach at Lake Michigan. Tom groaned and rolled over, one arm flung over Joanne's bare midriff.

Did he make a deliberate move or was he sleeping? *I like the feel of him, his bare arm on me.*

A tentative touch of her hand to his brought a gentle response. Tom slid welcoming fingers on her bare skin. *Lower, go lower,* she thought and opened her eyes, saw families too close for comfort, a stray ball coming their way, a small child running after. All thoughts of carnality washed away in a day at the beach.

Rising wind prevented the raft from happening. Disappointed, Joanne said, "Will there be a next time for he beach?"

Tom folded the beach towels and repacked the ice chest. "Definitely next time. There's an outside shower at Haven. Beats driving back all sandy. What do you think?"

"I say thumbs up." She gazed a long lingering moment at the beach, curls of waves forming at the shore with parents beckoning small kids into their own Haven. She'd seldom experienced love and care. Abruptly Joanne turned away at so much perfection not meant for her.

"Nice day, huh?"

"Oh yes."

On the drive back to Old Town, Tom said, "I have a question about, uh stars."

"Stars?" Joanne glanced sideways to see if he was serious.

"The little stars on your swim suit. Are they permanent or did some fall off in the lake?"

"Are you serious?"

"Yes. Definitely. It's a valid question." He held up a hand. "Nothing personal."

"Hmm. I didn't count them or buy with a guarantee. Counselor, can I get back to you once I've done the necessary research?"

He cleared his throat. "Over dinner, tonight?"

After a whole day with him, I'd love to spend even more time. Dare I take a chance? No. Don't spoil a good thing.

"Little louder, please?"

A time for her to ask questions. "Tom, do you have secrets, dark ones you can't share?"

"Everyone keeps secrets, Joanne but the answer is no. I shed most of mine like a snake out-growing my body on New Years' day when I had an epiphany and realized I had to change. No dark secrets were buried." He stopped at the first toll booth, collected the ticket and continued driving. "I'll take a guess and ask if you're talking about yourself; you can't or won't share secrets or maybe you haven't met the person you can trust to tell."

"I'm locked up with my secrets, Tom and as much as I'd like to, um, be closer to someone, you, right now I can't. Understand?"

Tom nodded. "I'm here whenever you need me" and said, "I love being with you."

I want to cry. But I'll wait 'til I'm in the apartment alone with my gun to remember the man who damaged me maybe beyond repair when I came to this city alone and he pretended to be a friend.

At the curb to her apartment, Joanne felt the touch of Tom's hand against her cheek wet with tears she didn't plan to let escape. Damn the tears. He drew her close and she didn't flinch. His lips touched hers. Reaching up, Joanne ran fingers through his sun streaked hair to pull him tight. The kiss intensified with the wonder of tasting each other for the first time. He pulled away.

"Are you trying me on for size? If so, I hope I fit."

Unbuckling the seat belt, she opened the car door and reached in back for her beach bag. "This day was perfect because of you. I *will* try to open my heart. Not easy after locking up eight years ago. See you tomorrow"

Walking up the stairs, she heard Tom's car radio playing an oldie, "Am I Blue, am I blue?" Yeah, poor guy. He probably was.

Chapter 26
Charlie

Heart pounding with one thought in her mind, "God, let him be all right," Charlie jumped out of her car, forgot to close the door and raced up to Haven. Fumbled with the key, dropped it twice, finally opened and caught her breath. Too quiet. Frantic, she ran calling his name. "Jerry, Jerry" and found him in the bedroom, a smile on his dear face, arms open wide to greet her.

"Hi, Love." He dropped the book he'd been reading on the floor and patted the bed.

Charlie knew the look, what the old sexy expression meant. Since the accident, the look had gone along with so much of him. With high heels kicked off, a suit jacket flung to a chair followed by everything else she wore in her business persona, Charlie climbed on the bed naked and snuggled with her husband.

"Tell me everything about Shelley, the..."

He nuzzled her neck. "Later. First I want to show you how pleased I am to ..." Guiding her hand down his chest and further down in the nest of curly brown hair, stood a major erection.

"Let's get re-acquainted, my darling."

She leaned forward, the scent of vanilla lotion, her favorite fragrance, strong on his body.

He sighed. "A hello kiss might be nice."

"Your wish is my command and you smell so good. I bet you taste at least as delicious. Um, we haven't, since, so don't take too much time because..."

"Hello handsome, cum here often?" feeling wicked as she licked his hardness. With a firm hold at home base, Charlie opened her mouth, heard Jerry say, "Sit on me, no time to wait."

"Won't I hurt you?"

"I don't think so. Try, Charlie. Try."

Carefully she straddled him, poised above his erection and slick with her own juice, eased her way down. "Jerry, I've missed you so much. Can you feel me?"

"Yeah, oh yeah. Now slide up and down squeezing tight. Oh, just like that. A few more and I'm..." he gasped, "Charlie..."

Hot sperm filled her just the way she'd dreamed of. Maybe this time, without planning like two scientists, they'd conceive. *Shush,* she thought. *No distractions.*

When he caught his breath, Charlie rolled off and tucked her head under his chin. Married eight years and this was a major moment; hopefully a return to a happier life together.

Holding hands, they lay side by side quiet for a while, no other sound than the shutters rattling when the wind picked up.

"I didn't pleasure you, did I?"

Charlie burst into laughter. "Bet you will and soon, knowing you." Changing position, she laid on her side to prop one elbow under her chin. "I didn't hurt you in anyway, did I?"

"No. far from that. I feel like a man again. It's been a nightmare all these months believing I'd never be able to pleasure you, feeling worthless. And today, you should've seen me helping with the birth, a guy helping his friend, team work and me a part of it. It gave me confidence and a lot of bruises."

"I wish I could have been there to see my guy in action taking charge. Jerry, you're the only man in the world I want to be with, ever. I love your mind," she kissed his forehead, "your eyes, nose and mouth,' and kissed those parts paying special attention to his mouth and tongue, and got carried away with caresses and kisses down to the growing length of him.

Her voice, husky with desire, said, "What time are the kids coming home?"

"About five."

"Hmm. Just enough time for one more shot." Charlie threw her head back and laughed at their private jokes.

"Climb aboard, sweetheart. This time we finish together."

After a quick shower, Charlie sat on the edge of the bed dressed in a tee shirt and shorts aware Jerry watched her every move.

"What?"

Her husband had a satisfied after-glow on his face. "Remember the night we celebrated your birthday and..."

"I said I was a virgin and removed my new summer dress and you said you were, too..."

"And we made love for the first time."

"Yes, we did."

"Are we glad we waited?"

"Yes, we are."

Chapter 27
Three weeks later
Joanne

Intense with research for another lawyers' case, Joanne answered the phone with a curt, "Joanne McKenna Friedman here."

"Tina Endicott here, Joanne. You learn fast." The smoky voice of the big boss's secretary/receptionist gave a throaty laugh. "We must do lunch one day. Do lunch. That's a stupid expression, isn't it? I always thought one ate lunch but that's me. Anyway, George Arnold's new client requested you as second chair for his case. I don't know any particulars but trust me, I will and soon."

"I don't get it. Nice to have someone ask for me but why and what's his name? The client."

"This is a heads-up. Don't get your panties in a twist until I call again."

Did she say panties in a twist? Such a friendly unexpected call from Tina Endicott. I never thought Ms. Gorgeousness could be warm and funny. You never know.

She returned to the tedious job of research for yet another lawyer. Some day, after paying her dues, Joanne would be the one who assigned projects to associates. A florist knocked and delivered a dozen red roses. The day brightened with Tom's card. ***Thinking of you and a certain day at the beach. Rafting, anyone?*** Later she'd call and say yes, Yes, YES!

The Catch

The day didn't end as expected. George Arnold called for a meeting in the conference room on the 18th floor at five. Arriving on time, Joanne entered to find the lawyer seated, a drink half empty in his hand.

"Sorry if I've kept you waiting, Mr. Arnold."

He waved away her comment and gestured to the seat across from him.

"Cut the formality, Joanne. Call me George. What's your pleasure?" He pointed to the liquor cabinet. "Help yourself."

Before taking a seat she strode across the room, aware of him watching her, opened a small fridge and removed a bottle of Perrier. Poured a glass full of the so-called choice sparkling water and returned, sipped and waited.

Emptying his glass, George, her new best friend poured, another from a bottle labeled Chivas Regal. Scotch, Joanne recalled. Dark liquid and he drank it straight. Hmm.

"Are we waiting for anyone else?" The room could easily accommodate fourteen or more.

"It's just you and me, kid." He glanced over as if this were some kind of test. "You don't carry a tape recorder, do you?"

Surprised at the question, she opened her bag, found the small device she always carried and placed it between them. "It's not on. Why did you think I'd record our conversation?"

"I always take precaution." He drank deeply, swallowed, smacked his lips. "Goes down easy, Joanne. Try it sometime." Tie loosened, first few shirt buttons undone, he leaned back in his chair. "You're wondering why you're here so I will make an attempt, in my present state, to reveal the case you'll be involved in."

Joanne kicked off her heels, wiggled cramped toes and leaned forward, a feeling of foreboding crept over her. She wished George weren't half in the tank; wished she were with Tom at the beach; wished she were any place but here.

"I've known, let's call him John Smith for now, John since childhood. Kindergarden. We were best friends, families close, like that. I noticed odd things about my pal as we grew up; mean spirited acts like throwing rocks at cats and dogs, then hurting kids on the tennis team who played better than he did like tripping a nice kid and stomping on his ankle 'til it broke. He claimed he slipped on wet towels and couldn't stop his fall." The glass and the bottle of Scotch were empty. He tried to squeeze a last drop by holding the bottle upside down and tapping. Tap, tap, tap.

Joanne glanced at her watch, not pleased to find an hour passed and she still didn't know what the hell this had anything to do with her.

Appearing to be lost in retelling an old story, George went on. "John and I went separate ways in high school. His reputation was that of a weirdo and I had plans for law school. S.A.T's, good deeds and sports added up. While at Harvard, I heard he was making a lot of money but never found out how until he contacted me about an investment guaranteed to make a bundle. Joanne, check the liquor cabinet for another bottle of Scotch, preferably Chivas."

She didn't move. *I am not a lackey here or anywhere*, she thought.

"Joanne, uh, please."

"All right but please continue. I must get going."

One last bottle of Chivas delivered, he opened and drank greedily from the bottle like a hungry infant. "Insider trading. I needed the money and didn't think of the consequences, so I got money from my folks, with a promise I'd pay it back. They trusted their golden boy and I trusted," he paused, seemed to search his sodden mind for the made-up name, "John. Last week he called in trouble with something else and threatened blackmail. He said he'd kept a folder on me and ..." Palms up, a bleary eyed George stared at Joanne. "He specified that you be second chair. I don't know why. Tomorrow, meet up here at noon and I'll go into as much detail as possible. And Joanne, this is completely private information. One word gets out and your career at Bancroft is finished."

Dismissed with his words ringing in her ears, Joanne slipped into her heels, picked up her handbag and left. What the hell just happened? The eminent George Arnold drank too much, maybe revealed too much, and turned it around with a threat. Joanne shivered in the elevator glad she was alone. Everything she'd worked for could go up in flames if she spoke to someone and she ached to confide in Tom needing his warmth and friendship. *Did Tom know deals existed in this fancy law firm? He's been here longer than me and a smart guy like him...I've heard of scandals in law firms but believed Bancroft far above others. Maybe not.*

Out in the fading late summer day, she took a deep breath, listened to the seductive call of Lake Michigan and stepped to the curb to hail a taxi. A freshly washed yellow cab, water still dripping, pulled to a stop and weary, Joanne climbed in, gave her address and sat back for the ride.

From now on, I carry my gun everywhere. I've been threatened and who is this John Smith? I've got a bad feeling about the case. Damn. Just when I thought it was safe to go into the water...

She fingered the scars, rubbed them as if they could be erased along with memories of how they got there. The cab stopped. She paid and tipped the nice driver who'd respected her privacy, or maybe he had his own problems to think about. Hand in her bag on the Lady Smith, Joanne hurried up the steps, opened the mail slot, grabbed a handful of envelopes, and strode to her door. At last, safety. Tom deserved a call for the beautiful roses. It seemed so long ago and actually she inhaled their fragrance in the morning. Collapsing on the couch, she called him.

"Thanks for the gorgeous roses. You're spoiling me."

"Not as much as I want to. How was your day?"

Floodgates opened. Joanne cried and couldn't stop.

"What happened? I'm coming over." He broke the connection.

Oh God, what a wimp I am. I hear Tom's voice and cry. And I can't tell anyone or I'm finished.

Joanne hung up her suit, blouse, tucked new shoes in a bag and dressed in shorts and a big tee. She tied back her hair and washed her face. A knock at the door. Tom. And she didn't have time to apply concealer. *Shit. Who cares.* Barefoot she ran to the door and looked through the security peephole. Yes, Tom's rugged face marred only by a worried frown. Joanne cleared the locks, flung the door wide and fell into his arms.

He kicked the door shut and held her without speaking. Guiding Joanne to the couch, he sat and pulled her on his lap.

"What happened, honey? Tell me. I promise, Scout's honor I will never repeat what you say. Are you ready to trust someone? Me?"

Joanne gazed into his blue eyes filled with nothing but truth; no hidden meaning there, and no guile. Never except for Poppa had she seen eyes so pure.

"Yes, Tom. But I have to warn you, it's not pretty and it's about our law firm."

He inhaled and exhaled slowly. "I haven't eaten. Have you? Bad news might sit better if we've had something."

"Eggies?"

He laughed. "Perfect. I'll whip up two omelets and then we'll talk."

After crisp bacon and cheese and spinach omelets, they cleaned up the small kitchen and returned to the living room.

"Want to sit outside?"

"I'm afraid to." Joanne hugged a pillow to her middle and told him about the private meeting with Mr. Arnold, call me George. Leaving out nothing, she ended with the threat to have her fired if she disclosed their conversation. "And he scheduled another meeting for tomorrow."

Silent for a moment, Tom stood up and paced the floor. "In my department, I've found mostly envy, no threats, graft, or anything evil and what you're telling me smells like evil. George Arnold is in the upper echelon of the company, top defense lawyer and he's successfully defended some nasty characters. That's straight from Channel Gossip." He sat next to Joanne, guzzled down half a bottle of water and shook his head. "First he asks you to sit as second assistant to that bogus case. Why you? A newcomer at the firm over some hard working associates who'd put out to be in a courtroom."

"Put out? You don't think I ..."

Planting a kiss on top of her head, he laughed. "Of course not. But getting ahead can be like the casting couch in show business. Some people feel they have to compromise in order to get ahead. And that goes for men as well as women."

Smiling Joanne glanced up at Tom with his blond hair, blue eyes, wide Irish cheek bones and square jaw. "So, did you put out, Mr. Donnelly?"

He tackled her right there on the couch, kissed her lips as if they hadn't kissed before until she parted her lips and for a little while Joanne forgot about threats, evil, the law firm and enjoyed the physical pleasure of new romance.

"Joanne?"

"Yes."

"Joanne?"

"I said yes and I mean it." She held his hand and felt like skipping down the hall with her soon-to-be-lover. Excitement grew when Tom lifted her big tee shirt over her head and gasped.

"I didn't expect...you looked different in the sparkly swimsuit. You're so petite, um dainty." His big hands cupped her white lace bra. "Lace. Oh, thank you."

Her shorts pulled down easy and there Joanne stood in a transparent scrap of lace panties almost naked. *The moment of truth is nearly here. Naked means scars and burns revealed. He cares for me. I trust him. I may even love him.*

"Tom, you're fully dressed and I'm almost naked. How come?"

"Are you in a rush to see my football scars, wounds from years of being tackled, kicked, punched and jumped on?"

He has scars, too! "Hell yes. Take it all off, big guy."

Off came the sweat shirt, shorts, sneakers, socks. She knew what Tom looked like in swim trunks, the six pack abs perfection, the Adonis of him. Jockey shorts protruding in front aiming toward her was another matter.

"Are you ready for us, sweet heart?"

He calls me sweetheart. He loves me. HE wants to make love not get laid.

Holding out her arms to Tom, Joanne gave her wordless answer.

It had been a long time since Joanne was in bed with a man. This one, Tom, smelled good, a spicy musky scent guaranteed to give a woman, well supposedly guaranteed, excitement. And he did have scars which he displayed with a sense of pleasure.

"This one came from the quarterback from Purdue who managed to run over me with sharpened cleats, I bet," Tom pointed to a long pale line.

Joanne ran a finger over it, licked her finger and repeated the gesture. She pictured the young football player cut and bleeding through his jersey always toughing it out.

"I wish I'd known you back then, Tom, wish I'd seen you play football with bands, cheer leaders and crowds. I never had the experience."

"We have now."

Her eyes closed, his mouth found hers, the warm pressure sent desire rippling through Joanne. His hands slid around her back unhooking the lace bra. "Sweet," Tom whispered licking her nipples.

"You're experienced, Tom. I, well I haven't had much so teach me, okay?"

Hot thrusting rhythm of his tongue in her mouth stoked her until she glowed like burning embers. Joanne reached for him frantic with desire. She heard a packet tear, a shift of position as he used protection. *So soon. Is it ending so soon?* Deep inside she felt hot moisture rise, rhythm beat against— inside her sex.

"Are we ready? I can tell you are, know I am."

"Oh, yes, yes."

Serious now, Tom guided himself into her velvety core, slow at first and then with an urgency that carried them away. Exquisite shock waves rocked them and after a long while the world drifted back into focus.

"Is this where we light up two cigarettes?"

Tom, still on top and inside, almost laughed. "I don't smoke. Neither do you. I do have a suggestion, though."

"Hmm?"

"Let's wait a while and see what comes up?"

"Oh, Tom." They remained in bed, Joanne not moving, Tom's eyes closed. "Oh,

Tom, honey. Oh."

As he predicted, something came up.

The next early morning over cereal and milk, Tom had a suggestion. "If George doesn't ask about your recorder, tape the meeting. I have a high tech super small recorder you can hide in your bag. Leave your bag open on the desk facing him, both recorders turned on. Make sure you have fresh batteries. As King George VI said in 1939 when Britain was on the brink of war, "Keep Calm and Carry On." Actually it was a propaganda slogan never issued to reassure the population they would be defended at all costs." He grinned showing a dimple. "This is your war, Joanne, today. We'll discover who the enemies are and fight and win."

"Tom, the more I get to know you, the more I really, really care for you."

"On that happy note, I'll race home and change clothes. Share a cab to work?"

"Why not? I'll be downstairs at 5."

As Joanne applied make-up, she realized her skin glowed this morning. It must be true, sex plus love made a difference.

Chapter 28

After a tight hug and kiss in the cab, Tom and Joanne strode into the tall building.

Shoulder to shoulder they waited for the elevator, greeted lawyers as a crowd surged behind and around them, everyone eager to begin the day. Joanne felt Tom pinch her thigh just before he left as a vote of confidence. Nervous she rode up to her office. The appointment was for noon.

She hoped Mr. Arnold would be sober.

Concentration came hard today. Threats bounced around in her head and she scribbled Keep Calm, Carry On, over and over and thought about Tom making love, his body, their bodies together, and wondered how he knew so much about King George VI or was it just one bit of information he carried in his memory bank.. And once she wrote Joanne Donnelly. *That's it. Enough with the foolishness. FOCUS and get ready for the conference.*

Stomach clenched Joanne tried to finish a granola bar, a swallow of water with every bite. She brushed her teeth, hit record on both recorders and rode up. This time she waited. And waited. Turned the little recorders off and on when almost an hour in the empty cold room the well known lawyer breezed in.

"Looking young and tasty today, Ms. Friedman."

Right off the bat he opens with a case for sexual harassment caught on tape?

"I'm looking forward to more information, Mr. Arnold." Her laptop was open to Word ready to take notes.

"Close that immediately." His eyes narrowed and she almost smelled fire and brimstone in his aftershave.

Dell shut down. Joanne listened.

"Does the name Morton Goebel mean anything to you?"

Icicles formed in her veins. *Breathe in, Breathe out. Keep Calm, Carry On. The naïve young girl inside Joanne woke up and screamed. The girl who trusted the kind man when he said he'd make her dreams come true. He'd help if she'd be nice to him and later a friend or two. Gave her a clean room in his big bachelor pad, he called it. Call me Morton. Call me Morton when he burned her with cigarettes; call me Mr. Goebel when he cut her.*

"Yes." The new improved Joanne McKenna Friedman sat taller.

"He's the John Smith I referred to yesterday. Is there any reason he'd ask for you to be second chair?"

She held herself together. "What's the case about?"

"Morton, my best pal from childhood, is being sued by a young woman who claims he used her for prostitution purposes, pimping her to his wealthy friends. And he wanted her to get girl friends involved, she says. There's not much to the case except she has hospital records of serious assaults paid for with his insurance. He says he took pity on the small town girl and is shocked by the claim. Old Mort is holding a threat over my head. Remember I told you yesterday about the insider trading deal where I made a lot of money with Mort's help?"

How can I forget? Joanne thought. "Yes, I remember."

"He says if I don't win the case, I'm going down with him. As for you, Ms. Friedman, he wants you to be ready to testify as to what a decent person he is. How he helped you when you were new to Chicago. Understand?"

The implied 'or else' hung in the room. *No wonder the eminent lawyer figured he could call me tasty. He thought I'd been a prostitute in my previous life. Well, guess again.*

"And you expect me to validate his lies? I thought truth is what law was all about."

A laugh burst from Mr. Arnold. "Are you really naïve or is this an act? If it's an act, you're good. Very good. Mort said that after a little instruction you were very good indeed." He leaned across the wide conference table. Joanne smelled breath mints covering a foul mouth.

"We're associates here at Bancroft, Joanne. True I have seniority but when you cooperate, the ladder to success comes," he paused and winked with the word 'comes', "faster."

She wanted his proposition on tape. "What exactly do you mean by cooperate? I've been helpful with research, worked endless hours on that other case, I'm always on time. What more can I do to prove how valuable I am to the firm?"

If this weren't so serious, I'd bat my eyelashes and pretend to be a complete dope. Spell it out, you arrogant son-of-a-bitch.

Smoothing his power red tie, his eyes gave Joanne what she figured was a smoky gaze with heavy lids, knowing smile.

Oh geez! He's a walking cliché, this big shot.

"Dinner, wine, a room for two where we can get to know each other intimately. You're such a looker. I'd like to see you without the suit. Do you wear little satin undies? I love satin. Makes me hard just talking about it. Come around to my side of the table, Joanne. Now."

How do I get out of this? Just segue back to the case.

"Oh, well I think we should discuss Mr. Goebel's problems uh, first and how to solve them before going to court. May I have access to the plaintiff's statement? This will require diligent research. I'm a research specialist, at least that's what Paul McCann said when we worked together, for you."

Writing furiously on a yellow pad, anything to divert the great lawyer, Joanne figured out a way to escape. With a furtive move using her left hand under the table, she texted Tom asking him to call her asap and say emergency. Make up a story fast. Get her the hell out of this room.

Some of the starch left the stiff lawyer on the make and he shuffled papers in his briefcase as she babbled on.

"Sorry. Hi, I'm super busy in conference. What, Oh, no. I'll come right away."

The Catch

"A problem?"

Joanne scrambled for her bag and stood. "Sorry. A friend is having twins, too soon, labor. I have to go. She's like a sister to me. I'll make up the time. Thanks for everything."

And she flew out the door into the next elevator and out to fresh air where Tom waited around the corner where no one could see them.

"C'mon. I have lunch, water, the works. We're going to Haven where we can talk in peace. The recorders worked?"

"I hope so. Tom, Arnold's disgusting and this case is scary. Remember I mentioned secrets?"Tom's brow wrinkled. "On the way back from the beach."

"Oh, yeah. You said you had a terrible secret. Does this have something to do with the case?"

"I'm having an emotional hemorrhage right now."

They got into the next cab in line.

His arms went around Joanne. "Hang on. We'll stop at Old Town, change clothes and go. Shush."

She ached to spill the awful story, knew it would have to wait. Keep calm and carry on. *King George VI, seems simplistic. Guess it worked. Eventually the war was won.* Closing her eyes, she dozed wrapped in Tom's arms.

Tom drove right to the beach, deserted this warm late summer afternoon. Lake Michigan lay placid, the dark cold water a mystery. After devouring tuna sandwiches followed by chocolate chip cookies, Tom wrapped up the napkins and took Joanne's hand. "Time for a walk."

It's much easier to spill when you don't have to face your best friend. Holding hands, they kicked the sand and walked the wet shoreline. "Picture this, Tom: Unhappy at home, I ran away at seventeen and headed from Missouri to Chicago. Right away I got lucky with a job slinging hash at a diner. The owner got fresh; I was a tough kid and he never tried it again. I saved my pennies because I didn't have much money. My goal was to get a real education. I dreamed of being a lawyer and that required a lot of money." She stooped, made a sand ball and pitched it as far out as possible and watched it fall and break apart in the lake. "This is a condensed version, understand." Tom nodded.

'One night as I walked to the bus stop, I stayed at the Y during this time, a shiny black car slowed next to me, the window rolled down and a man smiled and offered me a ride. Well hell, I was innocent, tired, a ride sounded good. With no loving folks around to say don't talk to strangers, I got in. He said his name was Morton Goebel. The rest is nasty so I'm going to tell you and if you hate me I understand. He seduced me by taking me into a luxurious world I didn't know existed. Suddenly I had new clothes and went to school where everything was paid for. All I did in exchange was to have sex with him. And later he introduced two of his very best friends who added to my growing college fund and when Morton Goebel asked if I had girl friends...I ran."

Bending down, Joanne scooped up another handful of wet sand, formed a ball and hurled it into the lake. Dimples formed on the smooth surface of the water as the sand disintegrated.

"C'mon." Tom held her sand covered hand and marched to the blanket. "Sit close to me." She moved over an inch. "I'm sad to hear about your past. Joanne, you were young with no one to guide you. I grew up sheltered, kind of spoiled and made a mess of my life. When we have kids we'll teach them not to talk to strangers and keep them busy with sports." He looked out toward the lake for a moment. "About this case. We need the advice of a top attorney, one we can trust and I know him."

"Outside the firm?"

"Way outside. Charlie's uncle Stuart Alfred. He's the man if I can reach him and if he remembers me."

"A lot of ifs."

"Tom, did you say when we have kids?"

He grinned. "I guess I did."

"Are you asking me to marry you even after all I've revealed and even though we just met a couple of months ago?"

"Uh huh." On one knee he gazed at her, tucked a few errant strands of dark hair behind her ears. "Joanne McKenna Friedman, will you marry me?"

Tears streaming down her face, Joanne nodded. "Yes, Thomas Donnelly, I will marry you. What time?"

A kiss sealed the promise and when the kiss became serious with tongues tasting and bodies in contact, a whistle blew. The return of the lone life guard brought an abrupt halt.

Laughing they waved to him, shook out the blanket, gathered their picnic gear and raced to the car, kicking up sand all the way.

In the car, Tom used his cell phone to find Stuart Alfred's number.

The great attorney picked up. Tom recognized the educated voice of the older man.

"Mr. Alfred, You probably won't remember me. I am Thomas Donnelly."

"Do not ever do me the disservice believing an old coot like me forgets...anything. How are your parents, the fair Bridget and your rascal of a father, Patrick Senior?"

"Fine, sir. Thank you."

"Now cut to the chase. I am in the midst of mayhem here and my treasured secretary says she has the flu, in summer. Preposterous, isn't it? She probably needs a manicure or something feminine."

"Sir, I'm a lawyer with Bancroft ..."

"Stop with the Sir and yes, Bancroft, what a bunch of scoundrels. Go on."

"My fiancee is involved in a case that reeks of threats and lies."

"My schedule at the office is booked. Come to our home, tonight at seven, for dinner. You and the lovely..."

"Joanne McKenna Friedman."

"Good heavens. She delivered our latest grandchildren on a hillside at Haven. Wait until Eleanor hears who's coming to dinner. Prepare for the red carpet, young man." Connection ended

"Did you hear any of the conversation?"

"Honey, you had it on speaker phone. What an interesting man and funny. So he's Jimmy and Charlie's uncle and grandfather of all those children."

"Yeah all that. Um, actually the Alfred's took Charlie in when she was fifteen and later did the same with Jimmy. Long story. And wait 'til you see their digs. His wife is beautiful and they're in love, those two. A real romance."

"From your description I want us to be like them."

"My folks are similar."

Joanne sighed. "Do we have to dress up?"

"Oh yeah. Our best duds short of formal."

A mental inventory of her wardrobe came up negative. "Is there time for me to shop?"

"Only if you're fast."

Joanne gave a wicked chuckle. "You know I am."

Chapter 29

At the last minute, Joanne tried on the perfect dress. Silk raspberry with a faded flower pattern, ruffled front, covered buttons, graceful short sleeves and a wide skirt. She thought garden party, twirled around and bought it on sale. Black strappy heels would suffice with sheer hose. With her hair pulled back and some curled tendrils around her face, she was ready to go when Tom rang the bell.

"My fiancée is magnificent. Perfect."

"And I'm happy to hear all those good words from my fiancée. Have you told your parents?"

"Not yet. No time. Tomorrow is soon enough. Right now we're going to Lake Shore Drive. Do you have the recordings and your notes?"

Patting her bag, she nodded. "I'm slightly hysterical and all set. Should we bring flowers or candy?"

Tom furrowed his brow. "Hmm. I remember Charlie saying her uncle loved some very fancy chocolate and her aunt loves flowers. They have two huge Labradoodles."

"So Peppermint Patties won't do?"

Tom threw back his head and laughed. "I love you."

"There's a specialty chocolate shop three blocks east and a flower shop next to it. Let's stop."

Parking, they hurried in both drawn by the chocolate aroma. "What's the finest chocolate, preferably dark?"

"Ah." A man dressed in a fine suit rubbed his hands together. "Come this way." He led them to a counter where a small selection of chocolate truffles were displayed. "These are the finest truffles in the world from Belgium."

"I'm speechless. You pick them, Tom. Maybe ten and put them in a gift box. Thank you. Hurry."

Selecting four filled with dark crème, four with vanilla, and two cherry filled, Tom put on a happy face and paid a bunch of money. Off to the florist where Tom bought his special roses, this time a mix of yellow and pink and half an hour later they parked in front of the Alfred's home.

Tom pressed the button. Chimes rang and a tall man dressed in black answered the door.

"Mr. Thomas Donnelly and Joanne McKenna Friedman."

"Edgar, you remember me."

"One never forgets."

"Ms. Friedman is my fiancée, Edgar."

"So she is." He turned away as one of the most elegant women Joanne had ever seen floated down a winding case.

"Your guests have arrived, Mrs. Eleanor."

"Thank you, Edgar. I can see that."

She embraced Joanne and kissed each hand. "These hands safely delivered our new grandbabies." Turning to Tom, she beamed with a smile that could have lit the city. "You, Thomas, came to the rescue. What a team. And now word has it from my dearest you are engaged. How lovely. And what have we here, candy and flowers. This adds to the perfection. Thank you."

Joanne felt a light touch on her shoulder. "Your dress, dear. Wherever did you purchase it?"

Woman talk, what fun, she thought. "We live in Old Town. I found the dress in a shop on the main drag and on sale."

"I do love a good sale, don't you?"

Charlie looks a lot like her.

Edgar appeared. "Dinner is served, Madam. The Mister is grumpy with hunger."

Smiling sweetly, she said, "Inform him I shall not enter until he escorts me as is our custom. And please place these marvelous roses in water. Notice the absence of thorns. Chocolates in the study and Edgar, not a one to be missing before we've had a chance to dine."

The head of the household, attorney Stuart Alfred appeared. He was about five feet ten, had a slight paunch and shock of white hair, Smiling he held out a hand to shake with Tom and embraced Joanne in a tight hug. "Welcome. Eleanor, my love, my arm."

They entered a dining room fit for a movie set. Ivory damask cloth, not a wrinkle in sight, with matching napkins folded to stand like swans. Edgar pulled out chairs, poured wine. Another man, they called him Robert, wore a white jacket and ladled lemon soup with bits of rice, delicate and delicious. Eleanor asked Stuart about his day listening to every word it seemed to Joanne, and he replied with courtesy. She directed conversation to them, asking about Tom's career and how he and the Anderson's were getting along. Tom had to shake his head.

"You remind me of Charlie and her memory. She never forgets anything."

"She is gifted with a photographic memory, you may recall. That's how she managed to get her scholarship to NU. I have the same facility."

"Joanne, you were first Charlie's office manager and also went to night school. How did you ever learn to deliver babies?"

Joanne felt heat rise in her cheeks. "Mrs. Alfred, it's not exactly dinner conversation. Another time?"

"Of course. And call me Eleanor."

Dinner of sliced chicken with a light wine sauce, steamed spinach, and roasted red potatoes shaped like mushrooms went smoothly with Robert, a smile on his attractive face, not missing a beat.

Mr. Alfred pushed back his chair. "Now to the study. Eleanor, please join us. We have a most delicate private case to discuss. As always, I value your opinion. There is a guest bath room for those who wish to wash up. I will leave a trail of bread crumbs for you to follow. Also Lord and Lady will join us. They keep secrets."

"Lord and Lady?"

Tom grinned. "The Labradoodles I mentioned before we arrived. Family pets Charlie raised."

Joanne grinned back. "More and more I love this family."

Awed by the study with book lined floor to ceiling shelves, dark wood paneled walls and an attached ladder to reach everywhere, Joanne almost forgot the purpose of the evening. Tom steered her to one of the butter soft leather chairs and they waited until the Alfred's were settled.

"Let's see what you've brought to the table, Thomas."

Clearing his throat, Tom said, "This is Joanne's case. I'll let her explain."

The embarrassing moment of truth arrived. Face it and move on.

Step by step, Joanne explained the plaintiff's case as she knew it at this point; the similarity to what she'd experienced about nine years ago at the hands of Morton Goebel; threats to her and to George Arnold. "I taped the conference with Mr. Arnold today at noon. If you'd like, I'll play it for you now.

Eyes closed, the elder attorney smiled. "I'd like."

"And so would I." Eleanor patted her face with an embroidered handkerchief. "So much evil, my dear."

Loud and clear, the recording clarified the situation Joanne found herself in. When it ended, Mr. Alfred's eyes opened wide.

"Do I smell chocolate?"

"A gift from our young guests, dear. You are allowed one after dinner. Dark chocolate Belgium truffles, your favorite." She passed the plate around to the foursome.

"Delicious." His wife leaned over, handkerchief in hand to dab a tiny speck of chocolate from the corner of his mouth. "Thank you, dear. Regarding this pseudo case, Mr. Goebel is a fraud and worse. We have enough evidence to crucify him. But this will never get to trial. When you depose the plaintiff, there will be enough evidence for the defendant to want to settle. This is our goal. You do not want to lose your job under a cloud. When you leave Bancroft and you will,"

Stunned by his words, Joanne interrupted. "I will?"

His hand raised to stop further questions. "For a more reputable firm, you want your record to be unblemished. Once you are free and clear, we attack the bastard. He is a predator, a pimp and deserves a lengthy prison sentence."

"Eleanor, I need another truffle to get through all this difficult brain exercise. Please."

He savored the final truffle and continued. "Ask Sean to bring the dogs. I also need a bit of their love."

She rang a bell and magically two huge fluffy dogs thundered in, a young guy hurried close behind. They snuffled around Tom and Joanne, sat when Sean gave a hand signal, tails wagging, smiles on their intelligent dog muzzles and finally lay down at their master's feet. "Thank you, Sean. Do you have a ride home?"

Sean, a Down Syndrome boy of indeterminate age, bobbed his head up and down, a lop- sided smile on his face. "Yes, please and thank you, Mister. Robert takes me."

"Good night. See you tomorrow, my friend." With a contented sigh, the elder lawyer said, "I will write a script for you, Joanne. If you follow it to the last word, we'll nail the son-of-a-bitch and that goes for that pompous ass, George Arnold, too."

"Stuart, your language is appalling tonight."

"I can't help it, my dear."

"How can I get this to you in strict confidence tomorrow, Joanne."

"I can pick it up at your office. My schedule is more flexible than hers. Name the time."

"Eleven the latest. Are you agreeable, Joanne or do you feel railroaded by me?"

Joanne rose and crossed to his side. "I'm overwhelmed and grateful, Mr. Alfred." She sniffled and suddenly the embroidered hankie was in her hand. "Thank you both for everything."

"Our pleasure. I'm going to enjoy this. It's a far cry from some of the boring law I've practiced the past few years.

Outside, they paused. Tom pointed across Lake Shore Drive. "The lake is across the street. Running paths, a zoo, the beach, bicycle paths, everything free."

"And Charlie lived here. How amazing."

They settled in his car both still excited about the evening. "What a night, huh? I never dreamed Mr. Alfred would jump in the way he did" Tom turned the car around to head west.

"And what a couple. Funny, clever, smart and they've been together forever, I bet."

He squeezed her hand. "Just the way we'll be."

They traveled west in silence when Joanne asked how Tom knew about Charlie's early teen years and how come he used the expression 'taken in' by the Alfred's.

"I'll make a long story short since we'll be home in a half hour. I saw Charlie the first time when she came to my high school with her uncle. A new girl with the famous lawyer." At a red light, Tom glanced at Joanne. "Too much information?"

"You began at the beginning and you're painting a picture the way a writer does. Hmm. Lawyers do that. Anyway, go on. The lights green, honey."

"Never thought about it. Maybe I'm wasting my talent in writing boring documents for wealthy clients."

"Don't quit your day job, Tom. Now tell me more."

"Okay, spoil sport. Then she outran everyone on the track team and stood her ground when the girls were mean. The football team called her Speedy. She didn't talk to anyone. Just studied and ran. We dated at NU for one week and broke up. Since I've been helping out at Haven on weekends, she wanted to get re-acquainted. Her idea. And she filled me in on how she left home at fifteen, came to Chicago to meet her aunt and uncle."

"Like me except I didn't have family."

He pulled over, kissed her with so much passion Joanne wanted to unbuckle the safety belt and make love right then. Sighing, she motioned for him to go on.

"Have I told you lately that I love you?"

"Hmm."

"Thought I'd mention it. To continue: The Alfred's didn't have children and welcomed Charlie as if she were their own. When her brother Jimmy wanted to visit, again they opened the door to him. Raised a difficult cowboy to be a responsible loving son and husband. "

"Thanks for telling me. I envy them. On the other hand, I have the best catch of all. You."

She kissed him at the curb and said goodnight. Tomorrow promised to be a busy day.

Chapter 30
Shelley

"We still haven't named the babies, Jimmy. What's the matter with us?" Shelley rocked in the worn chair, a baby nestled in each arm sucking away at bottles. They were four weeks old, the first feeding frenzy slowed a little as they grew and grew. Jimmy swaggered in, remnants of shaving cream evident on his neck.

"It's 'bout time, ya think?"

"Yeah, I know."

"Any ideas?"

"Of course I do. Joanne delivered them, both Jerry and Tom assisted. I'd like to honor them somehow."

Jimmy folded long legs to sit on a braided rug next to Shelley and the babies. The nursery smelled of lotions made for new tender skin once again surrounded them. Now there were six children to love and care for but first the new babies needed names. "Joanne is a pretty name. Or how about Jo?"

"Jo Costigan." Shelley rolled the name around on her tongue. "Or Jo Lee, Jo Lynn, Jocelyn. Oh hell. Jo it is. No middle name. Everyone will think she's a boy."

"Not when they see her auburn curls down to here." He patted Shelley's behind.

"No, my husband. We've fooled around quite enough. How about our latest son?"

"Tom and Jerry."

They laughed, the babies burped.

"Terry Costigan."

Over a lot of laughs, Jo and Terry were named. As far as the parents were concerned, it was signed, sealed and delivered. A baby naming ceremony came next.

In his expert way Jimmy changed the twins and spoke to them as he gently smoothed his favorite baby lotion over little limbs and massaged saying, "So big, you're growing so big."

Shelley loved his routine. She'd watched and admired him from the first set of twins. When he finally told her how he and Charlie, ages four and eight, cared for their twin sisters, her heart broke. *Imagine a four year old changing, feeding, and bathing infants.* Shelley and Jimmy's first boys were twins four years old.

"Terry and Jo?" Charlie shrieked with laughter when Shelley called. "Shel, this is great. You covered all the players. How are the newbies today?"

"C'mon up. We're receiving company, girlfriend. And Jerry? How's he doing? I'm ready to begin our sessions again."

Through the phone a sound reverberated in Shelley's ears. Thump, Thump. "What's that?"

"My husband. On crutches. Feet touching the floor." Charlie's voice broke.

"You're crying. Get up here, all of you right now. You must show off for this worn-out Momma."

Jimmy patted little Jo and two long strides brought him to his wife's side. "What happened, Sweetheart?"

"Jerry's on crutches. He's on his feet. Jimmy, it's a miracle."

His muscled arms surrounded her. "You're my miracle, darlin'."

"You sweet talker." They kissed and she pushed him away. "They're coming over. It's your turn to break out cheese and crackers and eggs. Uh, boil a dozen and I'll make egg salad and please gather some tomatoes from the garden. Rinse them and slice, not too thin and..."

As he loped down the hall to the kitchen, Shelley heard him grumble and she grinned. Her capable man always turned funny playing the beleaguered husband.

"Just 'cause I sweet talk the woman she expects miracles from me, blah, blah, blah."

A sense of satisfaction washed over her. She needed time for make-up and a change of clothes, then back to life as Shelley the friend, psychiatric social worker, and mother of three sets of twins.

Uh, something's gotta give because I am not Wonder Woman. Jimmy and I will figure it out.

The purr of an engine stopped, Emma unbuckled her booster seat and ran in careful not to slam the door. Two sets of twins tumbled over each other, happy to see their cousin. Jake and Lucas whispered, "Babies sleeping." Dawn and Amelia, three years old, mimicked their big brothers.

"Careful, honey." Charlie's voice sounded nervous.

"I'm good." Thump, thump went the crutches.

Shelley stifled the impulse to assist when she wanted to rush to his side. "Hey kids, nice of you to stop by. We've made a feast, egg salad," she held the door opened, "your favorite, Jer," he thumped in, sweat running down his face, "and look at you. Bet some sweet iced tea would hit the spot."

Jimmy caught him before Jerry dropped the crutches and his legs gave out. A weak smile from Jerry was his reward and he settled his brother-in-law on the couch, pillows behind his head. "When Shelley said get the fuck out of the wheelchair, you listened."

"Hey, you had to. She's scary."

"I know. She's my wife. Shelley runs a tight ship."

Charlie brought a glass of iced tea to Jerry and wiped his face with a cold cloth. "One Dr. Pepper coming up, Jimmy."

"Thanks, Sis. You okay? You look a mite peaked." Charlie exchanged smiles with her husband. "I'm cool, bro."

Hot dogs were served to the kids on the porch and Shelley carried a Lazy Susan revolving tray out for the adults. In late summer with cicadas a buzz, Monarch butterflies floating everywhere attracted to the sweet bushes Jimmy planted, and tiny hummingbirds pausing to drink nectar while they beat their wings in quick time, life was idyllic.

"Listen to the pond grow into a small river as it flows down over the boulders."

Charlie tilted her head, long auburn pony tail over one shoulder. "Yeah. Like music. You and Jimmy have a symphony going on up here." She beckoned to Shelley. "Come with me, just for a sec." They strolled around the porch gazing out to the flower beds and woods.

Charlie leaned against the fence, a satisfied grin lighting her pretty freckled face. "We did it. And it worked."

"When?"

"Four weeks ago, the day you had the twins. And Shel, we did it a lot and I'm almost positive I'm pregnant."

"Oh, I'm so..."

"So are we. Don't tell anyone, except Jimmy. That's a given, until we're positive."

Filled with joy and possibilities, the families had a wonderful afternoon.

Chapter 31
Joanne

The following day after the exciting dinner at the Alfred's had left Joanne spinning with what came next, she shared a cab with Tom.

"I'll call Mr. Alfred's office, find out if he's prepared the um, script for you and if it's ready, I'll pick it up. Can you break away for an hour, meet me somewhere. I know a small bistro on Wabash. Nearby. Not a lawyers place."

"I may look calm but inside I'm a wreck. I'll make an excuse and get the hell out. Make it close enough for me to wear sneakers and walk. Tell me the name, call to say hi and hang up. That's the signal you have the papers. Then I'll leave."

"Manny's." Tom kissed her and they said a nervous goodbye in the elevator.

Manny's turned out to be an easy walk three long blocks south. Joanne strode along fast, d glad she wore a swingy skirt and light cotton shirt for comfort. Catching her reflection in the shop windows, she thought she looked like a shopper with nothing on her mind except clothes. No hint of a lawyer in her persona today as she was about to nail another lawyer and wreck some lives in the process. *Shit. What kind of a rotten person am I? Damn. Poppa, are you watching me? I'm fighting serious issues here.*

Tom waited just inside the door and escorted her to a booth at the back of the small restaurant.

"My stomach's in a knot. I don't think I can eat."

"Mine, too."

He ordered shrimp cocktails, grilled chicken with lettuce and tomato and dressing on the side and just cold water.

"Okay?"

"Okay." She opened the long envelope. "It's a real script just as he said. My name with words to say and a space for the woman I'll be speaking to like Q and A. And he explains how to gain control of the deposition. He writes that Mr. Arnold expects to be in charge and I should say because I'm a woman, she'll be more forthright with me. And here's a big one: Demand privacy."

"Good plan."

Shrimp cocktails arrived. Joanne, into reading, forgot she couldn't eat and dipped the shrimp in sauce. "Delicious." Four jumbo shrimp were gone as she read and ate. "The man's a genius."

"He's been at law for a lot of years. Genius is his reputation. I knew I wanted to be a lawyer and my dad always talked about his old pal, Stuart Alfred, the smartest most honorable attorney in Chicago."

"How old were you?" Joanne tackled the grilled chicken.

"Hmm. A young teenager. Patrick had his sights on the police force like Dad."

After lunch they kissed and Tom took a roundabout way to the office. Joanne used her long legged stride returning fast and refreshed her make-up before anyone called. With the door to her small office closed, Joanne memorized Mr. Alfred's script repeating the lines over and over. One of the law classes she'd taken compared lawyers to actors and referred to scripts they must learn, absorb, and make the words live. *I won't have any trouble with this. I have lived her story and know what she's been through. We'll make him pay.*

Some yoga breathing was needed so Joanne sat still, her eyes closed, hands in lap palms up and breathed in through her nose to an eight count, held for eight and exhaled through her mouth for eight. A sequence of five times happened before her mind cleared.

The intercom buzzed. "Mr. Arnold wants you in the conference room, now."

"A please would be nice."

Marci at the desk laughed. "Yeah. Sure. Hey, do you love Pulp Fiction? Remember the scene where Mr. Wolf gives orders for the big cleanup and Vincent, he's played by John Travolta—I love him, don't you?-- says those exact words."

"I haven't had the pleasure and now it's on my To-Be-watched list. Thanks, Marci. And if you repeat this conversation you know what I'll have to do, don't you?"

"Uh, kill me?"

"Bye bye."

Joanne locked the script in her desk, turned on the tape recorders in her bag on the chance George was waiting and strode to the elevator bank with more confidence than she had the day before.

The bleary-eyed man, eyes suggested lack of sleep or booze, slumped in his chair and peered up at Joanne. His appearance was a far cry from the pompous self-assured lawyer of a few weeks ago when they first met.

Joanne sat and waited.

"Well, what are we going to do?" His voice was hoarse sounding desperate.

"How soon may I depose the plaintiff? That will clear the way and get things moving. She'll show me the hospital records and we go from there. What's her name."

The lawyer fumbled with a file, dropped it, picked it up and slid the file across the table. All the bluster gone from him like a fire burned out.

"Thank you." Page by page, Joanne read about bruised back, a broken ankle, black eye, fractured nose and rope burns noted in each injury. Shivering she fought to keep her composure. Sally Enberg. Pictures revealed a disheveled girl, about sixteen of Swedish heritage. *Farm girl runaway?* Blond, blue eyes, high cheekbones, undernourished in the photos. *God, Morton Goebel had turned into a worse monster than before.*

"And Ms. Enberg's lawyer? Who is representing her?"

He slid a card across the table. Franco Rivera. "I don't know him."

"He's downtown.

"I'll call Mr. Rivera and set up an appointment. A good plan is for me to speak with Ms. Enberg privately. As a woman, I'll appear to be more sympathetic. Anything further, Mr. Arnold?"

He shook his head and slumped even deeper in his chair.

"I'll give you a full report when I have something. And Mr. Arnold, please take care of yourself. You aren't looking well."

Hypocrite bastard, she thought riding down, *and isn't it wonderful.* She turned off the recorders. Not much on there except for her flawless debut. She called Tom."Do you know Franco Rivera, lawyer?"

"Yeah, I went to school with Frankie. Great guy. In private practice. What's your interest?"

"Sally Enberg is the plaintiff. He's her lawyer."

"Huh. He's tough. How did the conference go, my girl?"

"I give me an A+. Mr. Arnold has deteriorated fast in a short time."

"Scared shitless, I suppose."

"I'm going to call Rivera now to set up an appointment for deposition. Tom, I'm carrying the ball."

"Go for a touchdown, Sweetheart."

"Franco Rivera's office. Whom may I say is calling?" Joanne pictured a sexy woman with lots of make-up, gleaming black hair, lots of eye shadow. And cleavage.

"This is Joanne McKenna Friedman from Bancroft Law and Associates calling regarding his client, Sally Enberg."

"Hold, please."

"Franco Rivera here. Ms. Friedman your pleasure is to what?"

Joanne laughed. "That is a nice way to ask. I'd like to schedule a deposition with your client, Ms. Sally Enberg as soon as possible. Is there a window of opportunity on your calendar?" She heard flipping pages while whistling, *Takes Two to Tango*. Mental note. *He likes Ray Charles.*

"Today at four."

"I'll be there. By the way, Tom Donnelly sends greetings."

"Tommy! Many times he left me battered bloody on the field in football practice. Great guy. You know him how?"

"We're engaged."

"Mazel Tov. See you at four."

Chicago, a small town.

An attractive street front office greeted Joanne as she dodged traffic to cross Adams Avenue not far from Manny's. Big potted plants flanked the door with variegated marigolds filling a long box raised under the window probably so animals wouldn't use it as a sand box.

The receptionist, Sapphire Rivera, was exotic and young. Possibly the boss's kid sister or. . "Ms. Friedman, I presume?"

Joanne handed a card to her. "Your nails are spectacular." They were decorated with glittery stars and silver moons. Sapphire waved them in the air.

"My friend did them yesterday. I can give you his name and number, if you like."

A swarthy guy with a powerful build opened a paneled door. "Ms. Friedman, come right in." He smiled one of those TV whiter than white smiles advertising toothpaste that made a girl want to exchange spit with him. "Welcome to my humble digs."

Glancing around the spacious paneled room, Joanne noted it was at least as nice as anyone's office at Bancroft except for the Chief himself. *Humble, my ass,* she thought.

"This is very comfortable." She sank into a luxurious leather chair. A white fluffy cat with marble green eyes hopped on her lap. They stared at each other for a moment and the cat curled up; a purr began.

"Do you mind? Fluffy loves women and obviously you have a special scent. Oh, she doesn't shed."

Joanne stroked the cat and loved the feel of the warm body.

"Let's get right to business. Is Ms. Enberg coming?"

"Yes and soon. I thought we might sniff each other, figuratively speaking, please don't take offense, just to get a feel for expectations and begin."

"All right. Here are the facts I've learned coming straight from Bancroft. You represent a client who claims our client has abused and pimped her, an under aged girl, all under duress after making promises to take care of her and make this naive person a star on Broadway. This sounds like some worn out cliché of a sob story. Do you agree?"

Franco Rivera sat, hands folded and listened.

"My turn. We have a full dossier of hospital records which you have seen. Morton Goebel claims he paid all her hospital bills as a Samaritan. He doesn't know how she was injured or by whom. So it becomes He said; She said."

Here it comes, she thought. *The moment of truth.* "Mr. Rivera..."

"I will call you Joanne if that's permissible and please call me Franco."

"At this time, Franco, I want you to treat this meeting as if it were a confessional. This must be completely private until I'm ready to go public when my counsel agrees."

"And he or she is?"

"Stuart Alfred."

"Well, you knocked my socks off with his name. Look, the only way I can protect your privacy is if you retain me just for the duration of this mess. If you have a dollar with you, I'll accept you as a client right now."

Thoughts racing she decided to call Mr. Alfred and ask.

"I'm calling Mr. Alfred for advice right now. Please wait."

He left the room. Fluffy followed, tail held high leaving Joanne with a lap full of cat hair. *She doesn't shed, huh?*

When Joanne explained the situation, she pictured the great attorney absorbing information, eyes closed.

"Enough. Franco is a good boy, smart and savvy. Give him a dollar, tell your story and report back to me. You took command this day with Lawyer Arnold?"

"I did and memorized your script. Thank you."

"The script is now yours. Eleanor was quite taken with you, my dear. Next time you and Thomas come to dine, more Belgium chocolates would be appreciated. Perhaps twelve. Adieu."

She couldn't hide the grin when the door opened.

"Why a dollar? A retainer is always a large sum."

"I owe Tom and since Stuart Alfred is your counsel..."

"Change for a five?" She smoothed a crumpled bill.

He extracted four singles from his wallet and handed them over. "A formality. Something to sign making this official."

A few minutes went by before Joanne signed and had her own lawyer. Just in case...of the case.

Sally Enberg showed up soon after. Tall, slim and beautiful, the bloom of youth stolen by a monster. Joanne saw herself about eight years ago, not as pretty, vulnerable and easily led into becoming a willing victim.

Joanne had already played the recording of her conversation with George Arnold revealing her past connection with Morton Goebel. Nothing she'd say would surprise him so after introducing the women, Franco left the room.

"May I call you Sally?"

"Oh, sure." Sally crossed lanky jean clad legs. Joanne noticed she also crossed thin arms as if to protect her chest just like a pretzel all twisted. *I know how she feels.*

"Your lawyer gave permission for you to be open with me; to tell the truth with my promise not to hurt you in any way. Do you understand?"

She nodded, her eyes filled with tears.

"It's scary talking to someone you don't know isn't it?"

Tears fell as she nodded. "Uh huh."

"Would you believe I ran away from home when I was sixteen?"

"Oh my God, so did I!" Leaning forward, Sally touched Joanne's silk shirt.

"Where'd you get the money for this? Must've cost a bundle."

Laughing, Joanne said. "On sale, girl and you know what? I had a terrible experience that almost killed me. Lucky I got away and went to school. Now I'm a lawyer. That's why I'm here with you. Mind if I tape our conversation?" She removed Tom's sleek little high tech recorder from her briefcase and turned it on.

"Cool. Like on TV. Morty had one..." Color drained from her cheeks.

Joanne crossed to the small fridge in the corner and peered in. "Sprite, Diet Coke, water. Tea?"

"Diet Coke, please."

Waiting until Sally had a few pulls on the added straw, Joanne continued with the script, improvising as needed. "Morty? Do you mean Morton Goebel?"

Big blue eyes fastened on her. "You know him?"

"He's the man who tricked me into living with him and having sex with other men. I was a virgin, Sally and he tried to break my spirit. But he didn't know how tough I was inside."

Legs no longer crossed, Sally's arms waved around. "That's what he did to me only worse."

"Tell me how it started, step by step. Remember I'm a friend and I've been there. Are you hungry? I can order pizza."

"I like it with pepperoni and mushrooms and I'm starving. First I'm gonna wash my face to get this make-up off so I can breathe. Then I'll spill the beans, enough to cook the bastard."

Sally's sweet scent of orange blossoms lingered in the room. *Might she recover and have a full life after this experience? Maybe with therapy. Who knows.*

Joanne ordered pizza.

Ten minutes later an adorable guy delivered. An actor no doubt. He flirted with Sally. Joanne paid and tipped him on the heavy side. Spare nothing on this day to be generous.

Sally inhaled slice after slice. Joanne nibbled on one. The time to record had arrived.

Joanne began with the date, time, Sally Enberg , plaintiff in the case against Morton Goebel, defendant.

Franco's office smelled like an Italian restaurant, spicy sauces, hot melted cheese. Joanne wondered if he had a room deodorizer. If not, she'd buy one.

"Morty never let me eat pizza. Too fattening, he said."

"Where did you meet?"

"Huh." Sally wound a strand of blonde hair around one finger. "At Grand Central Station. See, I figured I'd get to New York and, well, I'd be there. Instead I'm in this giant place and scared shitless. Uh sorry. I didn't know where to begin, where the YWCA was and stuff like that. So all of a sudden this man, he looked like a teacher. Glasses, sweater, someone's dad, came over to me and smiled." Sally's eyes wandered around the richly appointed safe room they were in. "Why didn't I stay home where I was safe? No I had to run away. Adventure, be someone different. And look at me now." She rolled up her sleeves to show Joanne long faded yellowish purple bruises. "And that's just my arms. I ache everywhere."

Joanne handed her a tissue and fought the desire to kill the monster.

"I'm so sorry you've gone through this, Sally. It's over now. Can you tell me what happened next?"

After blowing her nose, Sally nodded.

"He smiled. He said I looked like I needed some help and he was a New Yorker all his life and could, if I didn't mind, make it easy for me to get settled. What a gentleman, a lot older than me, kind of like my dad. So we had a coke and talked at one of the little restaurants there and he bought a cheeseburger for me with fries. Hah. The last time I ate one of those. Too fattening. Next thing..." She stopped and ran to the bathroom where Joanne heard Sally throwing up.

Memories are supposed to be sweet.

When Sally returned, she was pale.

"Are you feeling better? Sometimes the combination of food and disclosure of unhappy events is more than one can bear. Take a deep breath, Sally and exhale slowly. You're doing a great job."

Patient, Joanne waited until Sally's composure returned. There was no stopping the young girl now.

"He had a Mercedes. Like a fool, I got in and we drove to an apartment. A big one, beautiful in a tall building with a doorman and everything. We went all the way to the penthouse, me with an old suitcase in such a super place. He said I could stay there rent free until I got settled. Joanne, I didn't question him! Geez. I should take a bubble bath he'd fix for me in a few minutes and get some sleep. That's when I had the first idea something didn't fit. Since when did someone have to fix a bubble bath for me? Like never. I locked the bathroom door and got undressed wrapping my old terry cloth robe around me almost thinking I'd shower in the locked room, when the door opened and there he stood, old Morty, a towel wrapped around his middle. "What the fuck are you doing here?" I shouted and that was the first time he slapped me."

Breathing hard, Sally paused for just a minute catching her breath and barreled on.

"Naughty word, he said and grabbed my arm, dragged me out of the bathroom to a sunken tub filled with sweet smelling bubbles. "Get in," and he pulled my towel away, licked his fat lips when he saw me naked and I had to get in. The bubbles felt nice, I cried, he felt me up, washed my privates and forced me to wash his. Disgusting. Scared, I did what he said, trapped like a rat."

Deep down Joanne shivered. "Can we get some fresh air? I need a walk around the block"

Together the two walked, one a woman, one a girl, both abused by the same man. Eventually they linked arms heading east toward Lake Michigan, the summer sky still blue and faded at days' end. Headlights of passing cars flashed by rounding the corner and there was the lake.

"Have you been to the beach?"

"No, not yet. When the bruises disappear, I'll go. I love to sun bathe even though I always burn."

"I have a good sunscreen. One day we'll go together."

Sally shook her head. "I'm going home where I belong when this is done. I left a boyfriend. Maybe he'll forgive me." She let go of Joanne's arm and turned away. "It's time to finish."

Franco lounged in a chair, reading. "You didn't leave a slice for me."

"Sorry, Franco. We were hungry and then decided we needed a walk. Sally wants to finish the deposition and get to sleep. When all this is finished, we'll go to the best Ristorante in town. My treat."

The young girl dropped into a chair like a rag doll. "I want to get this over fast as I can. Turn the recorder on, please."

Again Joanne added the time and date; Sally's name and the case against Morton Goebel and asked her next question. "After the time in the bath, did Mr. Goebel find work for you as promised?"

"Work?" Sally burst into tears and grabbed a bunch of tissues from the nearby box. "Work. Yeah. After a couple of weeks of indoor instruction on how to do it, he brought a friend, a man over to uh meet me. By now, I knew enough to listen and obey so when he had me dress up in a... like a Dorothy outfit from, you know, The Wizard of Oz, with the checked pinafore and little blouse and socks with kids shoes, I did. I looked in the mirror and couldn't believe I was Sally Enberg anymore. And Joanne, actually I wasn't. I'd changed into this skinny robot kid, like a wind-up toy." She took a time out for more tears.

The Catch

My heart breaks watching her relive the nightmare. I'm glad I'm here to help her get through it to nail the bastard.

"My job was to pretend I liked when the old man spanked me on my bare bottom. It hurt a lot. And I had to, you know, suck on his thing until...I threw up until Morty forced me to swallow. Later I saw the man give money to Morty. He never gave any to me."

"Sally, did Mr. Goebel enroll you in acting school? You said he promised to do that."

"Oh no. He bought movie magazines for me and had groceries sent in, all salads and what he called healthy food so I wouldn't get fat. And he made sure I exercised on his machines every day. Sometimes at night we'd go for a walk where he'd show me off to some friends."

"About the accidents you had during this time, when you went to the hospital. Can you tell me about it?"

"Yeah, sure." She seemed to search for a beginning. Joanne waited. "The first time was when he pushed me down the stairs and I had a concussion. He said I tripped and he tried to save me. When I didn't wake up, he had to bring me to the hospital. You have the records on all the times."

"Yes, I do."

"Well, it's documented and even though he says he was being a good guy taking care of me, paying the hospital bills, I swear to God, he's responsible for every injury to me in the past year until I finally had the guts to sneak away. And Joanne, I took my own clothes. That's all. I owe him nothing. He owes me my life."

Noting the time and date, Joanne turned off the recorder.

Sally scrambled for her possessions and ran out the door. Joanne sat motionless for a long time. Franco entered and broke the silence.

""She's back at her apartment. You look as washed out as she did. Can I get you a glass of wine?"

"Chardonnay, if you have it. Then I'll go home, call Tom and prepare to meet his family."

"You will break the news about your engagement tonight after all this?"

"Hmm. Yes." She tasted the cold wine and felt like taking a nap. Instead she savored every sip, munched a few cashews Franco poured in a bowl and set on the table and thought about what to wear to impress her future-in-laws.

"Thanks, Franco. It's been fun. Call me a cab."

"You're a cab." They laughed.

She walked outside to find a taxi waiting. *Another adventure lay ahead*, she thought and slipped into a power nap.

Chapter 32

Wearing the same pretty dress she'd worn to the Alfred's, Joanne, refreshed from a nap and shower, hurried to open the door when Tom knocked.

"Let's go. Can't be late."

"Hi Tom. How are you? My day was difficult and I'm so happy to see you."

"Sorry, Joanne." He kissed her and kissed her again as if he never wanted to let her go.

"That's more like it, big guy. You're pressured about introducing me to your parents. They don't know we've decided to marry, right?"

"Right. I intend to tell them tonight at dinner. All they know is I'm bringing my girlfriend over to meet them."

She reached up and held his face in both hands. "Tommy, they're smart. Why does a grown son bring a woman home?"

"Because he loves her and plans to marry her."

"Bingo." She kissed him with some tongue sucking. "How do I look?"

"Gorgeous except your lips need a touch-up and do you really need to carry your gun in your purse. Dad has guns. Patrick also never leaves home without one."

"Neither do I. It's hidden. Let's go."

Leading with her best foot forward, Joanne entered the cozy old home of Tom's parents. Bridget Donnelly greeted her with a hug. Joanne thrilled listening to the Irish brogue Tom's mother never dropped in all her years in America. And out lumbered a burly version of Tom, his dad, Patrick, Senior. She extended a hand to shake and was surprised when he scooped her small frame into a bear hug. *A powerful man*, she thought. *Was he scary? No.*

Joanne still held her bag so when he said, "You're packing, little lady?" she nodded.

"Protection?"

"Yes."

"It's every sane citizen's right. You know how to use it, I'm sure."

"I've been taught practice makes perfect."

"Always remember a paper target isn't human. Go for the mass if push comes to shove." His serious eyes met hers. "If you need advice, call me." He found a card in his pocket and handed it to her. "Don't lose it." A genial host, he escorted Joanne into a comfortable living room. Two old German Shepherds rose and made their way wagging furry tails. "Everyone, meet our Thomas's lady."

Joanne watched Tom morph into a son in the midst of a loving family, dogs and all. The scene enriched her picture of him. His brother Patrick, dark and handsome, so different from Tom, kept an observant eye on her or did she imagine. Melanie, his fiancée, a quiet pretty girl touched her dress reminding Joanne of Eleanor Alfred's questions about a sale.

"There's great shop in Old Town on the main drag. That's where I bought this, on sale." *Oh geez! Repeating bits of an old conversation to begin a new one.* It worked and they talked fashion and make-up, girl stuff until Patrick Senior called them to the dining room. Even the dogs came trotting.

"Mom, you roasted a turkey! It's not Thanksgiving."

"Tommy, me boy, I give thanks every day so why wait? You've brought a fair lass to our table. 'Tis a special occasion."

Touched with the sentiment and a fine dinner, Joanne lifted her wine glass. "I'll drink to that, Mrs. Donnelly. I'm so happy to be here."

"Call me Bridget, sweet girl."

The table groaned with the big turkey, gravy, sweet potato casserole, salad, and homemade biscuits. Joanne managed a little bit of this and that hoping no one noticed she was a careful eater. The two pets, tongues hanging out, sat under the table between the brothers waiting for scraps. Patrick Senior carved while regaling the family with obviously familiar tales from his days as a cop.

Tom comes from a nice family, warm and friendly. I can get used to this.

After dinner Tom rose and clinked his glass with a knife. "I have an announcement to make." He gazed at Joanne, his love palpable as the family quieted. "I've asked Joanne to marry me and she said yes." He pulled her up to stand next to him.

His brother's jaw dropped. "Where did you meet?"

Tom grinned. "We work at the same law firm, Pat."

His Mom and Dad clapped their hands. "Congratulations. Wonderful news. When did you meet and how soon do you plan to get hitched?"

Tom answered all the questions except for when they would marry. They hadn't talked about that.

Pat said, "What's your full name, Joanne? Tom keeps saying Joanne this and Joanne that."

"Joanne McKenna Friedman."

His parents stopped smiling.

"Is there a problem? My mother is Irish and Dad, Jewish. She lives in Missouri, Dad passed on." She turned to Tom. "What?"

His arm went around her. "If Joanne's mixed heritage bothers you, we'll leave and we won't return. Joanne and I love each other and we won't allow any prejudice to interfere. It can wreck a family."

Hold yourself together now. Joanne caught her reflection in the large mirror, face drained of color when a few moments ago she was so happy. If Tom's parents were like the Archie Bunker's from that old television series, she and Tom would turn their backs on them and lose a family. Without another word, they left. No one came out to yell, "Stop. We're sorry. Forgive us."

They were silent on the ride back to Old Town. Parking, Tom ran around to open the passenger door. Hands clasped, Joanne and Tom entered her apartment to shed clothes as they strode to the bedroom. Wrapped in Tom's arms, the only place she'd ever felt safe, Joanne sighed.

"And how was your day, love?" A feeble attempt to lighten the mood.

"I should have known or at least suspected their reaction."

"Why?"Tom pulled a light summer blanket up to cover them.

"My brother fell in love with Shelley Jackson first time he ever saw her. Pat came to watch me play an important football game at Northwestern U and there she was. Hot, gorgeous, and black Shelley was a basketball player and Charlie's roommate."

"Jimmy Costigan's Shelley?"

"You guessed it. Before she met Jimmy. They were in love, Pat and Shelley."

"So what happened and what's that got to do with us?"

"My parents didn't want their son bringing home little dark skinned grandchildren."

"Oh. I'm beginning to see the light." Joanne shifted position to watch her lovers face.

"So Pat strung her along until she told him to go away and never come back. By then she'd met Jimmy, younger but a guy with principles. He's someone I care about and trust. And that's their happy ending." They gazed at each other. "I love you and want us to be married as soon as possible. What's your feeling?"

"Right now, I'm feeling very good. You and I, love. Against prejudice and caving in. And something else I'm feeling." She reached down to find the object of her desire. Fascinated by his body since the day at the beach, Joanne couldn't get enough of him. "How about this time I get on top and see what happens."

"Not yet." Tom laughed. "Didn't you ever hear about foreplay?"

"That's for golf where a guy in pink shorts and a green checkered shirt hits a ball and yells "Fore."

They played but not for long when Joanne opened a jar of cream, dipped a finger in and anointed his erection. Up and down without friction she tightened her grip and straddled his lean hips. Leaning forward, she kissed him, their tongues performing oral sex. Too aroused to stop, she sat on his cock, slid all the way down, whispered to remind him, "I'm on the pill." They raced toward the climax building since they'd come home. To cum home again.

Once Joanne could think, she answered Tom's question. "Yes, Tom as soon as possible we'll be married. I'll finish this nasty case and get the monkey off my back forever."

Chapter 33

Shoulders squared, her way of showing strength, Joanne faced George Arnold across his desk. Food stained the red power tie he'd worn so arrogantly when she first met him not long before.

"What did you find out during the deposition yesterday?" He threw back a shot glass of Scotch. Ten in the morning and he was half in the tank.

"With Ms. Enberg's permission, I taped everything. She has a compelling case against the defendant. Shall I play it for you?"

Joanne turned the recorder on without waiting for his consent. Sally's voice came through loud and clear. Half way through, Mr. Arnold waved for Joanne to turn it off. He held his head in his hands and groaned.

"I'm screwed. My career is over. Morton is going to reveal my complicity in the insider trading scheme in all because of this girl's testimony. Isn't there something you can do, Joanne?

She clicked the on button to record his conversation with her. Not admissible in court but it might work out of court. "In what way? Can you suggest anything?"

"Money, a bribe to keep her quiet." He leaned forward, hanging on to his desk, whiskey on his breath. "I have a lot of money put away. Private stash. She could start over, go back home and forget about what happened."

"So you believe money would solve the Mr. Goebel problem? And what about his threat to me? Will money make my problem go away?"

Joanne saw in his blank expression the prominent lawyer had forgotten about her. She meant nothing to him.

"Oh, of course a financial settlement could be arranged. Uh,yes."

"Nice of you to include me, Mr. Arnold. I do have a workable solution however."

He brightened.

"Today at four, we'll meet in the conference room. Sally Enberg, her lawyer Franco Rivera, my counsel, the well known attorney Stuart Alfred, you and please arrange for Morton Goebel to attend. Everyone's time is valuable and we want to discuss the case before going to court."

Before he could say a word, Joanne gathered her belongings and pulse racing, she left to call Tom asap and report. The thought of meeting the monster face to face after eight years made her want to throw up.

In her office, she closed the door and called Tom from the new throw away cell. No taking chances now.

"I did it. The meeting is for four today. Everything's in place. Mr. Alfred agreed to meet me. He sounded positively gleeful. I taped Arnold's bribe offer you said he'd make. Tom, I'm nervous."

"About Goebel."

"Yes. Do I need police protection?"

"Hmm. I have a plainclothes cop friend. His name's Mark Lane. I'll call him right now and get back to you. He might be available or can get another cop."

Pacing didn't work off the excess energy so Joanne sat on the floor and concentrated on Yoga stretches. Tom called. "All set. Mark will come to your office as a prospective client and go up with you. He's armed."

"So am I."

"Tell him. I love you, honey and I'm so proud of you."

Now she could nibble on an energy bar, drink water and focus on the task at hand. She checked for fresh batteries. Ready or not, Morton Goebel was in for a big surprise.

Three thirty a knock at the door and a voice said, "Mark Lane." The tall muscular cop with longish brown hair wearing dark glasses, dressed casual, with short leather boots came in smiling. "I'm at your service. Tom laid out the situation. Is there anything you need to explain?"

"There are a few pertinent facts, Mark. I carry a gun and know how to use it. One man who will be at this meeting held me as kind of a prisoner eight years ago and abused and pimped me to friends. I ran away. Now he's done the same and worse to a young woman who will also be at the meeting. He's threatened that if we don't clear him of charges, he'll have me fired from this company. I don't think he'll try anything at the meeting but he's dangerous and guaranteed he'll be furious with the outcome."

"Okay, I've got it, kind of and I'm ready. My gun's tucked in my pants under my jacket in back. Another's in my boot along with a knife. I'll be your assistant, carry your bag and hand files to you. If there's any shooting, get out of my way. I'm an expert."

There came another knock. He spun around.

"This will be Stuart Alfred, my counsel."

Dressed to perfection, Mr. Alfred entered. He smiled seeing the cop. "Hello, Mark. I haven't seen you in a long time. Your parents are well?"

"Yes sir, Mr. Alfred. It's an honor to be in your company today."

"Yes, it is." He kissed Joanne's cheek. "You've done exactly as I expected, young lady. Let us move on to the adventure. Show no mercy, my dear."

The conference room no longer smelled of whiskey. An extravagant bouquet of spectacular pink and yellow gladiolas, purple hyacinths, fern and baby's breath perfumed the room. George Arnold looked almost as fresh as the flowers, *transformed by the event*, Joanne thought.

"Mr. Alfred and my assistant today, Mark Lane, meet Sally Enberg, Franco Rivera, Ms. Enberg's lawyer and George Arnold."

The men and Sally shook hands. She had dressed in jeans and a long sleeve silk shirt like the one she'd admired on Joanne the night before. Joanne gave her a thumbs' up. Sally almost resembled a teenager again. Given time, a supportive family would help her to recover. The damage had been done.

All the players were accounted for with the exception of one.

Joanne took charge. "Mr. Goebel is late."

The attorney fidgeted in the head chair. "We spoke last night, Morton and I. I told him about the meeting, time, place and purpose. He assured me he would be here." A check on his gold Rolex and his face showed concern. "He's never late."

"He is now. Almost fifteen minutes. Please call him."

The lawyer turned his back and obvious to everyone, he called. When he turned to the waiting group, George's face was pale. "No one answered, not even his voice mail. I called the desk. They said he left in a hurry early this morning after calling for a cab. They said he had some bags."

Joanne watched as Mark Lane rushed into action. "I'll get an all points bulletin out for him and trace the cab." He left.

"As you can tell, Mark Lane is an undercover policeman. I asked him to come today for protection against Morton Goebel. Sally and I had enough to worry about. Mr. Goebel is dangerous and now he's on the loose so my fears were warranted.

"Okay everyone. Settle down. We have a lot to discuss. Mr. Arnold, I have you on sexual harassment to me, bribery to a client and to me. That's just the beginning." He sputtered, held up his hands in what appeared to be protest. 'The other guy did it' defense. Joanne had him cold on tape.

"Mr. Alfred, what do you suggest?"

His benign appearance didn't give a hint to his brilliance as an attorney.

"Thank you, Ms. Friedman. These are serious charges, George. I'm not surprised since I've heard more than rumors of your sexual harassment to young lawyers. In some circles your behavior is called the casting couch syndrome. Some women succumb in order to succeed not trusting on hard work and talent. Smart women like Ms. Friedman do not. She used an old reliable weapon and taped you propositioning her." He held up his hand in a firm gesture. "This is not admissible in court. Therefore we meet in private. We don't want to involve Ms. Friedman in a he said/she said situation." Joanne poured water in a tall glass for him. He sipped some and continued.

"Your knowledge of Morton Goebel's statuary rape of two young women, kidnapping and prostituting of these girls is unforgivable. Since he isn't here at the moment, and he will be caught and found guilty of these heinous crimes, I have an edict regarding you." Stuart Alfred rose and stared at George Arnold. "You are to transfer two million dollars to the account of Sally Enberg immediately."

Sally's eyes widened. Again Joanne gave her a thumbs' up.

His fist pounded the table as if it were a gavel. Joanne sat up straighter and listened to every word. "You are to transfer two million dollars to the account of Joanne McKenna Friedman immediately. This is a small price for what you have done. And next and most painful to you: as we sit here you will send a letter of resignation to Mr. Hugh Bancroft stating ill health thus ending your career as a lawyer. Do that as we speak. I want it notarized in our collective presence."

Appearing to be shaken beyond words, George Arnold called for his secretary to bring everything Mr. Alfred required. Sally and Franco drank water and talked quietly to each other. Joanne squeezed her counsel's hand.

"You've taught me a great lesson about speaking out today. And the money..."

"Just bring the chocolates, my dear, tomorrow at seven. Eleanor cannot wait to see you again. There is much to discuss. And Thomas? He is well?"

"We have a serious problem with his parents."

"Ah. Prejudice rears its ugly head once more."

"Once more?"

"Eleanor and I know about our precious Shelley and young Patrick."

The Catch

The money transfer from an account in the Cayman Islands moved fast. Sally handed her small checkbook to Franco who relayed the account number to George. Franco said, ""This large an amount needs to be invested carefully to insure your future, Sally."

Mr. Alfred touched his arm. "Call me, Frankie. There's an associate of mine who is knowledgeable. He handles my account."

"Yes sir. Tomorrow?"

"Yes. And Joanne, the same goes for you. My associate will see you at my office tomorrow at four. Bring Thomas." He patted her hand watching like an eagle as her transaction went through. "Good. Are you wondering about the appointment I referred to?"

"As a matter of fact, I am. I'm grateful but how do you know he or she is available?"

"I arranged the appointment in advance, my dear. A large sum of money came with this meeting. We want it invested without wasting time. Let's call it experience plus intuition."

Next on the agenda came the letter. Tears in his eyes, George Arnold resigned his high position at Bancroft Law and Associates. A notary came in signed and stamped the letter and Mr. Alfred made certain a secretary came in to deliver it. The case closed for now.

They filed out and stopped in Joanne's office for a few minutes. "We're not finished until he's caught. Be very cautious." Joanne hugged Sally. "Maybe you should head back home once you've decided what to do with all the money."

"By tomorrow or the next day, I'll be home again. I've talked to my parents," tears welled up in her eyes, "and my old boy friend. They said they can't wait to see me. God, I pray it works out." She sobbed. "I'm such a baby, crying every other minute."

Joanne handed her some tissue and a business card with her private number written on the back."You're one of the bravest young women I've ever known, Sally. Please keep in touch."

Franco shook hands all around. "I can't believe you're so new to law and yet you pulled this off. Consider today a major coup, Joanne."

"I had the best coach."

Stuart Alfred beamed. "She did, indeed. I must warn you, Joanne. Goebel may fake leaving town but it seems to me he'll seek revenge. Have Mark or Thomas guard you. Actually Thomas isn't qualified so a hired gunman is best. Carry your gun everywhere. I'll see you tomorrow. Robert is waiting downstairs to drive me home. It has been a most stimulating afternoon."

Alone, she checked her cell. Tom left a message he wouldn't be back until seven or eight. He had an appointment with a new client in Lake Forest. Happy Tom's clientele kept growing, Joanne sat a moment to collect her thoughts. *How did my life turn upside down all of a sudden or is this the journey I chose when I ran away at sixteen? Who knows. One thing I've learned is when Tom and I have children we'll love and cherish them..*

With no rush to leave the office, Joanne kicked off her shoes and curled up in a comfortable chair. Lap top in hand she wrote her personal take on the meeting:

"Beneath Sally Enberg's exterior lies a frightened beaten teen. She'll need therapy. Look at me, the Big Shot. I never had help and look where I am; a lawyer engaged to be married to another lawyer and I bet if I scratch my surface, I'm just like Sally only older. Mr. Alfred, what a honey, saved my ass today. Led me in the right direction, taught me lessons I'd never learn from a book or in a lecture hall. And if I'm not mistaken, he manipulated the law and George Arnold. Wait 'til Goebel is caught. Mr. Albert will fry him.

Her eyelids drooped and soon Joanne gave in to sleep.

Startled awake by a slammed door nearby, Joanne checked her watch to find it was nine o'clock and time to go home.

Chapter 34

Waving thanks to her favorite cab driver, Joanne slid her hand in the bag and fit her Lady Smith where it did the most good, right in the palm of her hand, a perfect fit. She strode fast toward the entrance, and suddenly missed being greeted by the long gone doorman, the late summer air sweet with a hint of autumn. Almost full dark, she approached the huge old magnolia tree near the entrance to her building, always the last to shed gorgeous purple flowers and a great place to hide behind. Distracted from her usual vigilance, the scene in the conference re-played in her mind and she grinned. Proud of a job well-done, Tom needed to hear every detail. She couldn't wait.

A shadowy figure emerged from behind the tree. Joanne tightened her grip around the gun, slipped it from her shoulder bag and held it close to her right side out of sight as she'd been taught. A familiar voice called, "Joanne, all grown-up looking very tasty to these old eyes." She froze and suddenly she was transformed into the sixteen year old run-away alone in a new city. The passing headlights of a car illuminated his face for just a moment. *Not the monster of her nightmares.* Diminished either by age or memory, Morton Goebel looked average, evil hid inside and he had something in his outstretched hands. A thin band. A wire, coming closer. She blinked, looked again and smelled the old familiar musk cologne and something rotten. The pungent smell assaulted her senses. *Too close--WAKE UP, Joanne.* His breath on her face, his hands reaching over her head ready to... She squeezed the trigger.

The Catch

Trembling Joanne watched him collapse to the sidewalk. Blood pooled around him. Morton Goebel's empty eyes were still open.

With no one around she called 911and gave the address. Then she felt a card in her pocket. Tom's father gave it to her and said to call if she needed him. She dialed. "This is Joanne. A man attacked me. I shot him and called 911. Please hurry. I need you."

She gave the address and waited staying far from the man who tried to kill her, never checking see if he died; hoping he was dead. She smelled blood mixed with the perfume of magnolia blossoms moments before and wondered if magnolias would remind her of death from now on and wondered if he had taken away another bit of joy.

Suddenly a car screeched to a stop and Patrick Donnelly Senior was all heart and business just before the police came. He talked to the first responder after placing his jacket around her shoulders and taking Joanne to his car to sit and wait. "I'll handle this."

She heard his every word. "Me boy Tommy's engaged to her. This guy attacked her with intent to kill. The wire is still in his hands. Strangling is my guess. She's licensed to carry and trained to shoot. And she did at close range. I taught her to go for body mass and she did." He put his beefy arm around the other cop. "Here's what has to go down. Our girl's a lawyer, like me boy. No scandal, no pictures of her, no name. Just another attack of a looney on an innocent woman on the streets of Chicago. Low profile, hear me? And then we're even for your son's problems. Kevin's okay now?" The cop nodded, his unruly mop of red hair falling in his eyes. They shook hands and moved out of earshot.

The scene faded. Joanne closed her eyes. *It's over. At last.* Shivering uncontrollably, she started crying and couldn't stop until she heard Tom's voice and felt his hands lift her from the car to press her close.

His dad spoke to more responders in the confidential way he had. Tom explained his dad was calling in all markers. Finally Mr. Donnelly came to them. "Tommy, take Joanne to your apartment. An investigator has to talk to her, clear the decks but hurry before the nosy news show up. We'll bag him

172

and get out. No comment. Another night on the job in our great city."

Tom drove the few blocks west to his place at the same time they heard an ambulance pull away in the other direction. A water hose cleaned up the scene leaving nothing for anyone to report. A car backfiring noise in the evening? Yeah right. *So this is how it's done sometimes, when necessary to protect and serve. How will I ever get over this?* Joanne thought. *Never. Now it's a part of me.*

Detective Mike Sullivan folded his hands, no notes taken, no recorder in sight, and sat leaning forward on Tom's couch. "Tell me what happened tonight, Ms. Friedman."

Tom's Dad sat beside her and nodded his head.

"I left a cab, started walking to my apartment when this man came toward me," she stopped to sip water and catch her breath, "he had something in his hands, looked like wire and when he tried to put it over my head I..."

"Fancy garrote. Looks like piano wire with handles.

"Geez, Pat. Haven't seen one of those since..."

"Yeah. Move on. Don't get too specific."

"You carry a gun often, Ms. Friedman?"

Joanne was on safer ground now. "Yes."

"Why?"

"For protection because I walk alone and single women are easy prey. It's my constitutional right to protect myself and I do. I am licensed and trained."

"Good. If there's anything else where can I reach you?"

Joanne handed over a business card.

The detective shook hands all around and wished Tom and Joanne happiness in their future marriage. "So Patrick, we're clear now?"

"Good boy, Mike. Call if you need me."

Mike Sullivan adjusted his cap and lumbered out.

The Catch

A silence fell between the three in the living room. Joanne spoke first. "Thanks for coming to my rescue, Mr. Donnelly. Your card," she held it up, "saved me.

"Thanks, Pop. I don't have a beer for you but I know what you did and Joanne and I are grateful." He stuck out his hand to shake.

Pat grabbed his son in a tight hug that ended with a hard smack on Tom's back. "My years of the blue line tradition paid off like one hand washing the other. Joanne, you have my respect. You are a special woman." He puffed out his chest and strolled around Tom's living room. "Not easy bein' on the force, careful not to step on toes on your way up the ladder. I had ambition, always wanted to be a good provider for me family." Stopping to gaze hard blue eyes into Tom's kinder blue eyes. "Ain't easy but I done it. Kissin' ass, beg pardon, Joanne, to the brass, doin' favors. Tonight a lot of it paid off, for both of you." He rambled on. "Nice house for me boys to grow and your mother worked hard, too. So tough. And you Thomas, a lawyer makin' big bucks, your brother a detective engaged to the little blonde girl from nowheresville. Me Bridget and I followin' church rules and all. We're good Christians, we are."

"Pop, you and mom were awful when Joanne said she had a Jewish father. A good Christian follows the Golden Rule to do unto others as you would have them do unto you. Are you so prejudiced that you refuse to acknowledge her as my bride-to-be? You ruined Pat's love for Shelley Jackson but Joanne and I are getting married with or without your approval. And if you don't approve of us, that's it. I appreciate from the bottom of my heart all the sacrifices you and mom made for me and hope I can repay you in some measure. Thanks again for what you've accomplished tonight. As we say in sports, the ball's in your court."

They never looked back as the older man, face ashen, left.

Tom's lips were set in a hard line. "I never expected my love for you would cause a rift." Joanne waited and hoped for the best. He traced the thin line on her neck the garrote left before she shot Morton Goebel. "Thank God you're okay, love. I never want to lose you, ever."

"I love you just as much, Tom. Your dad pulled off a major miracle tonight, didn't he? I pictured myself in handcuffs, fingerprints, jail, disgrace. I'm exhausted from the whole damn day and Tom, I pulled the trigger, squeezed it and a man died."

"Better him than you, Joanne. C'mon we need a break. Eggies and wait 'til you hear about my new clients."

They shared a plate of scrambled eggs and toast, showered and Tom suggested she take the next day off.

After mulling it over, she shook her head. "No. I have a martyr complex. I've gotta tough it out. We're meeting Mr. Alfred at four to discuss finances. By the way, darling, did I forget to tell you I'm a millionaire?"

"What?"

"I'm way too tired to explain but it's true. Two million dollars in my account were transferred from a numbered account in the Cayman Islands courtesy of George Arnold. Hmm. The Caymans. Is that a good place to honeymoon?"

Tom slept. Joanne had nightmares waking time after time to reach over and touch the safety of his love.

Chapter 35

The beautiful Tina Endicott entered Joanne's office without knocking. She sat, a mischievous smile on her perfect lips and crossed endless legs. "I don't know how you pulled off yesterday's coup but girlfriend, I could take lessons from you and I've been here a long time."

Joanne played innocent. The conference meeting was private, supposed to be private unless the room had a bug planted. She hoped not. "Coffee, Ms. Endicott?"

Tina laughed. "I have spies, with hints of this and that. I put them all together and figured them out," she tapped her perfectly coiffed hair, "in my little brain. So here I am. Congratulations. What threw me for a loop is when word got around the eminent lawyer Stuart Alfred was with you. You, the newbie, a rising star especially since George Albert, that phony, sent in his resignation stating poor health. Yeah. He has more like a bad case of poor judgment."

Joanne couldn't help herself. She laughed. "And you are here...why?"

"Are you nuts? I want to follow you wherever your path takes you. I'm a great second. I'll be faithful, loyal and all the bullshit but it's true, Joanne. I may look ultra chic but I'm a down home kind of girl who wants to get ahead not as a lawyer . I have no designs on that but a second in command or whatever. So please, check my creds and keep me in mind for the future. And happy engagement to your hunk." Tina flew out the door up to the penthouse where her position was secretary to the head of Bancroft Law and Associates.

The Catch

What an interesting start to a new day, Joanne thought. *Who'd a thunk it?* She checked the morning news. No headlines about an attack in Old Town. Page four. There it was. A small column about another attack on a woman alone. Mention of the brave woman warding off the attacker. No names revealed of the dead man or the woman. No exact location. Old Town referred to as a large residential community north of mid-town Chicago. Women warned to be wary. Gun control fanatics screaming for legislation, others calling for more mental facilities.

As if anything could have stopped Morton Goebel. He wanted her dead; had a garrote. Oh God. Thank you.

Three thirty came at last and she let the head office know she had an appointment. Off she went to meet Tom and a financial advisor. *Joanne McKenna Friedman, you are a millionaire.* Out in the sunny afternoon on Michigan Avenue, the Magnificent Mile, with Tom at her side, Joanne felt as magnificent as the mile they walked on.

Later that evening after dinner, the Alfred's and Tom and Joanne sat in the lemon scented study where the Labradoodles snuggled close to Joanne. Lady laid her curly muzzle in Joanne's lap and Lord placed both front paws across her shoes in his protective stance.

She rubbed Lady's head and stroked her back. "Am I the honored guest for some reason?"

"To Eleanor and me you are, Joanne. The dogs sense a need for comfort inside you. They're following instinct."

"After we're married, I think two Labradoodles would be great companions. It was great having two German Shepherds when I was a kid. What's your feeling about pets, honey?"

"Hmm. I can't think about ...I feel fragmented with too many images barging in." She stroked Lady's ears, patted her back, and remembered "Keep Calm and Carry On."

Eleanor passed around Belgium dark chocolate truffles, twelve this time, on a silver tray.

"Having to kill someone in order to survive is a major trauma, my dear. You may need counseling or a wedding right here." Eleanor's husband of many years smiled an impish smile, selected a truffle and popped the whole piece in his mouth and chewed. "Ah, food for the Gods."

"Here?" Tom and Joanne said in unison.

Eleanor's laughter sounded like fine crystal tapped with a silver knife. "Of course here. Let's make preparations immediately. Is that all right? You haven't mentioned a mother. Is she around?"

Joanne clouded up at the word mother. *No mother for me.* "All right? It's the best. Tommy, is this okay with you?" He kissed her and nodded thumbs up. "There is the problem with his parents." *And I have none.*

"If they don't come 'round, dear, it's their loss. First what date works for all? We do want to take advantage of the season and changes and..."

As the women talked Stuart Alfred picked up the plate of truffles and beckoned to Tom. "Let's go to the billiard room. You play, of course." He went straight to a bar, selected a bottle of brandy, poured a snifter, offered one to Tom who declined and twirled the glass before drinking. "What date suits you, Tom? My calendar is booked. The middle of September is my first window of opportunity. The women have about three weeks to organize an intimate wedding. It can be accomplished without fuss. Our Mrs. Appleton will cater with staff assisting. Guests? I would like to see our children here. You and Joanne are friends with them. Did you know the new twins are named Jo for Joanne and Terry for you and Jerry?"

"Nobody told us. What a kick. Wait 'til my girl hears the news." Tom picked up an ivory cue stick, admired the beauty and chalked the tip. "I'm getting the impression you split the household decisions with Eleanor."

"The key to a lasting marriage is, Thomas, romance, compromise, more romance and one long conversation." Selecting another stick, he said, "Rack 'em up."

The men, serious during the games, sat for a respite over brandy for Stuart and Perrier for Tom. Ties loosened, Mr. Alfred became Stuart in the camaraderie of growing friendship.

The Catch

The older man sat back in a leather chair broken in over many years to fit his shape. "I've loved Eleanor since she was a bit of a girl, barely sixteen. We married after her coming out ball."

"Coming out?"

"Coming out is an old custom still in use in high society where available wealthy girls are introduced to equally available wealthy young men. The very word sounds archaic now, doesn't it? Tradition counts, my friend. Whether it's holidays, anniversaries, or just because. Perhaps the 'just because' counts more than all the rest."

"I'm taking notes."

"Let's see what the women have decided and we will..."

Tom said, "Compromise."

After another short time of laughter and pouring over notes, Tom and Joanne thanked their host and hostess for a wonderful evening. The women agreed to solidify wedding plans on the weekend.

Pensive on the way back, Joanne had to ask. "Do you mind dropping me off at my place tonight? I'd like to try sleeping alone just to see if I can fight my demons and win."

"I could sleep on the couch. Be close if you need me."

Reaching over, she kissed his cheek. "I've got to do this alone or else find a therapist." *Privacy. I need privacy. I have my gun. I don't need my gun anymore. Yes, I do. Protect, just in case.*

Old habits never die, someone once said and it's true, she thought. Joanne searched each room until satisfied, then placed the pistol on a ledge in the bathroom and stripped, careful to hang her pretty dress on a hanger and wipe her high heel strappy sandals. *Count your blessings, girl. The greatest guy in the world loves you as goofy as you are. All of a sudden you're a millionaire and you delivered twins on a path in the woods.* She closed her eyes picturing the scene: *she sees auburn hair, little head crowning, telling Shelley to push and breathe as she, Joanne, soon-to-be-Donnelly, catches the tiny newborn.*

She cried with joy, cried with sorrow, cried for all she'd lost and all she'd gained.

When the well ran dry, Joanne washed her troubles away and went to bed.

Chapter 36

Summoned to the penthouse, Joanne waited for what came next when Mr. Bancroft settled his portly frame in a comfortable chair close to her. *Too close for comfort*, she thought.

"You've heard the news about George Arnold, I suppose? He's resigned for health reasons. Frankly I had no idea he was in ill health. We will miss him. This gives you a step up, Joanne." He patted her hand.

"In what way? I'm so new here and just learning my way around the process."

Again he patted her cold hand.. *I hate his touch.* "You learn quickly. I've assigned you to assist another top lawyer. Donald Marcus. You'll like Don, I'm sure. Keep up with your continuing education and you'll go far." He grunted his way out of the chair and went to his seat behind the desk. The visit ended.

At the door Joanne turned and gave the boss her best smile. "I'm engaged to Tom Donnelly, another Bancroft lawyer."

His bushy eyebrows lifted. "How nice. Congratulations, Ms. Friedman."

Maybe this would end the patting.

In the elevator going down her stomach practically leapt into her throat. *Continuing ed? I just got my degree. Well, at least I slept last night.*

The Catch

L.B. met Joanne as she got off the elevator. He escorted her to the coffee room where the young staff gathered around the table. A cake decorated with "You caught the "Catch" of the year" was placed in the center.

"Let's see your ring," Angie, the receptionist said.

"Oh. We forgot all about a ring. Tom and I decided in the middle..."

"We can guess. Don't tell." L.B. grinned.

"Is a ring required?"

A chorus of female voices yelled YES!

Male voices groaned and everyone wanted Joanne "to cut the cake already."

"You really call Tom "The Catch?""

"Oh yeah. I've been here ten years and he never looked twice at me. Always polite but never the look you want." Angie sighed. "Lucky I met Leo on five. We've been married three years and we're good."

"Thanks everyone. This really surprised me. I'll save one slice for Tom." She turned to find nothing but crumbs. And the greeting on the cake had been squeezed on cardboard wrapped in foil lay smashed where the cake used to be. *Someone here is either jealous or doesn't like me. As Gilda Radner once said, "It's always something."*

Why can't life be easy? she thought and sailed back to her office as if she'd never seen the nasty sight. Two words for the son-of-a-bitch who tried to spoil a nice moment.

Over dinner, Joanne replayed the cake incident to Tom. He shrugged. "There's always petty jealousy in any office even at low income jobs. I hear about it all the time. Best thing is to mind your business, be pleasant, keep a low profile and ignore the rest. If you can't stand working in such an environment, consider another. Ribs are delicious." He wiped his chin. "Don't sweat the small stuff, honey."

"Hmm. You have a great attitude and experience. I'm new. Speaking of small stuff, am I supposed to get an engagement ring to make this official?"

Carefully Tom wiped his fingers with a wet nap. "Did you ever see the movie Moonstruck?"

She laughed. "Of course. Are you referring to the proposal scene in the restaurant? You already proposed on the beach and I said yes."

Tom got down on his knees right there in the "Best Ribs & Burger Joint" in Old Town. He looked into her eyes. "Will you, Joanne McKenna Friedman, marry me?"

"Yes, I will, Thomas Donnelly."

He pulled a small box from his pocket. She opened it. A sparkling diamond dazzled her. Tom slipped it on her third finger left hand. *A perfect fit just like them.*

"We're official then?" She held up her hand admiring the ring.

"Oh yeah." He kissed her lips tasting of barbecue sauce. "You're delicious."

"Listen up, everybody." Joey, the restaurant's owner called out. "This is the first proposal you ever seen here. Maybe there were others but none like this, huh? So drinks on the house, one to a customer, no under age, right counselors?"

"Right Joey and thanks. My fiancée would like a Chardonnay. More water for me."

Clapping began slow at first and built until the patrons shouted, "Kiss."

They did.

Late the same night Joanne opened her laptop and created a new document labeled Wedding.

"Now? Does it have to be right now?" Tom rolled over to gaze at his tousled wife-to-be.

"Yes. First your guest list. Keep it small."

"I don't know. Okay. My football buddies."

"All of them?"

"Well sure." He called off names from NU, eight strong. She could see his eyes light up with memories as he rattled off more names.

"Wait a minute. How far back are you going?"

"Oh. My pals from high school. Great guys."

"Tommy, you don't keep in touch with them, all of them do you?" She counted the names. "Small wedding out of control, honey."

"Hmm. I'm tired. G'night."

Joanne had no friends. No time to be one so the Costigan family, three sets of twins, Shelley's Grandmother and Marina Flores, and the Kahn's became the rest of the party. Tom might invite a few guys or have a bachelor whatever. His choice. Thirteen plus the amazing Alfred's who opened their hearts and home to them. Fifteen. We'll send an invitation to his brother and parents. If they decide to attend, great. Total nineteen. If not, two bad words for them. No bridesmaid stuff. I'll buy a simple, correct that to a simply gorgeous white dress, not bride but 'bridey' and maybe an old fashioned veil thingy so Tom can lift it to kiss me. A tear slipped down her cheek followed by more. She wiped away happy tears this time.

She had one more thought before shutting down. Catholic? Talk to Tom. Compromise. Maybe a Deacon. *Poppa, I'm getting married to this wonderful guy. Religion question. Help, please.*

Chapter 37

Middle October. One of the ten most beautiful days of the year according to the weatherperson. Potted chrysanthemums in red, gold, purple, and yellow bordered the spectacular garden at the Alfred's home on Lake Shore Drive. A white and yellow striped tent set up in the middle of the garden with seats for twenty two in place. Another canopied section was set for buffet dinner and tables complete with high chairs and children's paraphernalia close by. Song birds of every color twittered in cages added to a sense of nature and love in the air.

Upstairs in a guest room, Joanne, dark hair shining in soft waves around her shoulders, smiled at the reflection in the mirror of Eleanor zipping up her white dress. The surrogate mother she'd become in a short time smiled back. "This is my wedding veil." Eleanor unwrapped a tissue covered package and shook out a flowing veil.

Joanne gasped. "This is what I dreamed of."

Eleanor set the delicate piece in place and sighed again. "Wear it today. You can't keep it. It's to be handed down to Emma, Shelley's daughters, your daughters and so on down the line

You are lovely, my girl. Now I've married off three children. Stuart and I never had children and we believed our lives were perfect. One morning the door chimes rang and our lives changed forever for the best. First came Charlie and Joanne, she was just fifteen but what a girl. A few years later Jimmy showed up. Our boy was a handful and look how he turned out and Shelley, a dream. Six children," she paused to kiss Joanne's hands, "these hands delivered our little Jo and

Terry. And now we have you and Tom. I'm overwhelmed with joy and so is Stuart although he doesn't let it show."

Speechless, Joanne said nothing. She'd thanked her many times and today was the day. Edgar knocked. "Guests have descended upon us, Mrs."

"Do you mean the family has arrived, Edgar?"

"Yes. Like a plague of locusts. Roger that."

Joanne twirled around in new white shoes. "Does he always speak like that?"

"Like what?" Eleanor kissed her lightly on the cheek. "Wait until you hear the strains of Mendelssohn's processional and make a grand entrance. Someone will escort you outside." She appeared to float in a dress of autumn hues; swirls of gold mixed with brown and touches of red leaving a hint of orange spice behind.

Thank you for this day and all to come, God. And to you, dear Poppa, Thanks for answering last night.

Edgar's knock came and Joanne opened the door. A videographer captured her step by step where to her complete surprise, a smiling Stuart Alfred waited. "What a gorgeous veil. I feel as if I'm to be the groom." With his capable guidance, her butterflies disappeared as they walked outdoors. Eleanor handed Joanne a single red rose with white satin streamers, symbolic of Tom's love. Emma skipped ahead flinging rose petals to the guests delight. And at the end of a short walk down the aisle stood Tom wearing a tux flanked by two football buddies he couldn't leave out or they'd make him pay or so he claimed. His brother Patrick stood close behind Tom. This was a surprise and a plus in the mystery of families.

Deacon Collins began with a simple non-denominational ceremony. Tom knew him from law school and the concept worked for both of them. As long as he said, "By the power vested in me by the State of Illinois..." Yet when he came to, "Do you Joanne McKenna Friedman take Thomas Donnelly to be your lawfully wedded husband, to love and cherish from this day forward?" She wanted to shout from the roof tops, "I DO!" and managed to whisper, "I do."

Tom gave a hearty "I do," in response to the ageless question and whooped when Deacon Collins pronounced them to be husband and wife. Lifting the veil, he said, "There you are, my wife," and kissed her deep and hot.

They walked back down the aisle touching hands with all the relatives big and small, Emma still tossing rose petals with Charlie looking just a bit round and rosy trying to stop her. Jerry on crutches stepped over to shake hands and exchange kisses. Patrick stayed right behind them, one hand on Tom's back. And at the very end stood Tom's parents. Joanne took the initiative. She hugged them both and thanked them for coming. What a perfect time to heal the fracture.

"It's a fun bunch here and the food is great. I know everyone will enjoy your company. Stuart speaks well of you."

Bridget and Pat Senior exchanged glances and nodded.

"Yes, we'd like that very much. The wedding was lovely. Your dress is so pretty, different. And the veil, is it antique?"

"Eleanor loaned it to me just for today."

Pat's fiancée Melanie joined them. "Nice wedding. No big fuss. Maybe Pat and I..."

"We're having a big wedding with lots of cops. We have to. It's tradition. Be my best man, Tom, please."

Later when the newlyweds were having the first of the 'one long conversation' of marriage in Tom's bed, they agreed Happy Ever After with bumps along the way made for a real life.

"Not too many bumps, please dear wife."

"I can't guarantee it, husband mine."

Book Club Discussion Starters

The Catch
by Charmaine Gordon

- Are New Year Resolutions a good thing? If you decide to make one, what do you think about keeping it within your reach?

- Is it possible to let go of the past and free yourself to begin without dragging old wounds along?

- Community service is always a good way to cleanse your mind. Agree or disagree?

- In *The Catch*, Joanne and Tom work together as a team when Shelley needs them. This is a breakthrough for them. Joanne's skill and Tom's willingness to help make the difference. Can you, as the reader, foresee at this point the possibility of love?

- There is a lot of working through problems in *The Catch*. What do you think about Tom's reaction to his family's prejudice toward Joanne regarding her mixed heritage?

- Joanne relies on her gun. In this time of all kinds of gun control legislation under discussion, the right to bear arms is dealt with in *The Catch*. She is a licensed gun owner and trained so when her life is endangered, she's ready. Would you be able to defend yourself in a life threatening situat

More Great Books
by Charmaine Gordon

Sin of Omission

A twist of fate intervenes when Shelley keeps a secret that threatens to break apart the Costigans and her future. A mysterious client, Deanna Rose, enters Haven, victim of a savage beating under strange circumstances. Shelley investigate and finds Ms. Rose has an unsavory past. With the reputation and safety of Haven at stake, Shelley is at risk to lose everything and everyone she cares about.

Reconstructing Charlie

Charlie Costigan has a secret. Home life gone from bad to the worst when she protects her mother from another vicious attack by her drunken father. Midnight. Clothes thrown into an old suitcase, she races for the bus with a letter to an unknown aunt and uncle. "This is my daughter. Embrace her as if she were your own." Determined, Charlie begins again. Alone with her secret.

Now What?

I held his cooling hand and asked the two words spoken many times during our years together. "Now what?" This time there was no response. I was on my own for the first time. When my fingers touched his wedding ring, I slipped it off and held it in my fist. The gold band was warm. I clung to him. "Come back to me, dearest." Sometimes what you wish for is more than you can live with.

Starting Over

Each morning, Emily Kendrick runs on the hard-packed sand of St. Augustine Beach to clear her mind and heal her heart. From the widow's walk of the house perched high on the dunes, a man trains his binoculars on Emily...

To Be Continued

Elizabeth Malone wakes up the morning after an amazing night of passion with her husband of forty years to find a note: Dear Lizzie, it's not you, it's me. Abandoned by her husband, disappointed in daughter Susie's casual attitude Dad's having a mid-life crisis, Beth decides to re-establish herself as the winner she once was. When Frank Malone returns, he's in for a big surprise!

Meet Charmaine Gordon

Years of experience as an actor on daytime drama. Stage, spokesperson and commercials plus writing sketches for Air Force shows helped prepare me for the wonders of a writing career. Of course, I didn't realize it at the time when immersed in the written words of others, that I was like a sponge, soaking up how to construct a scene, write dialogue, and paint the setting.

My writing effort came later when I wrote a two page story, sent it to son, Paul who commented, "Cool. Can you write ten pages?" Seemed impossible but the story poured from my fingers and seventy thousand words later, I typed The End.

I kissed my acting career goodbye, leaving on a high note with the lead in an Off Broadway play, "The Fourth Commandment" author Rich Knipe. It was great fun and time to move on. Movies like "Working Girl", "Road to Wellsville" and having the pleasure of Anthony Hopkins company at lunch, working with Mike Nichols in "Regarding Henry" and singing outside with Harrison Ford, crying with Gene Wilder over loss on another set, When "Harry Met Sally" with the whole gang singing It Had to Be You. Lots of fond memories. My first job as stand-in leg model for Geraldine Ferraro in a Diet Pepsi commercial with Secret Service men guarding her and her daughters. A sweet time.